Paulene!!
Enjoy!

Bw

Dream Big Publishing
Byron Center, MI

Dream Big Publishing
A publication of Dream Big Publishing
Byron Center MI
Copyright 2015 by Johanna Marie
All rights reserved, including the right of reproduction in whole or in part in any form.
Dream Big Publishing is a registered trademark of Dream Big Publishing.
Text of this book is set in Garamond text size 13.
Manufactured in the United States of America
All rights reserved.

Summary: To become an angel, you have to die.
As fate should have it, your human death foretells your future. You can become many things when you die. Some become nothing and they peacefully move out of existence. They are the lucky ones. Others are not so lucky and join one of the races; vampires, demons or in special circumstances, warlocks. Some become angels. Angels of light; angels of dark.

Mostly it depends on who, or what, is there when you die. A vampire can turn you, and demons can twist you into despair just like them. Angels are different. Angels are supposed to be there when you die-- to gently guide you into your next life. Someone to help you along the way into darkness or light, so you don't fall from your path.

But not always. Every once in a while you are forgotten.

Sometimes you get lost. Stuck in a limbo between the dark and the light.

Sometimes the world forgets you for just a small time, but when they remember you...
it's too late.

I am Crimson. I am a Forgotten.

[1. Paranormal – Fiction 2. Romance]
ISBN-13: 978-1515133650
Johanna Marie
Copyright 2015 by Johanna Marie
All rights reserved.

DEDICATION

For Lisa and GREAT Aunt Moe, who helped give 'Titanium' wings

Chapter 1

I suppose most people start at the beginning. I try to forget the beginning. My beginning wasn't a bright white tunnel with a warm glow. It was red, deep angry blood red. Am I evil? Not quite. Am I good? My lips stretch across my teeth in a rare show of true emotion. Not quite good either. I suppose, I am smack dab in the middle.

I toss back the last shot in my bottle of whiskey and let the burn glide down my throat. I let the glass softy clunk back onto the wooden bar and stand. The bartender keeps his eye on me; they usually do. The Blue Room is crowded with the young and restless party crowd. Music beats outward loudly from a live band across the large smoke-filled room. The half naked teenagers scream into the microphone and hustle around the stage while the drummer pounds continuously on a shiny chrome set. The bodies in the audience sway rapidly against each other as alcohol and freedom loosen their joints and muscles. My feet want to pull me in that direction. I straighten my spine and put my hands in my back pockets. Another bottle and I would gladly be out there with them. I had never gotten to be the carefree young human adult. I had been turned at the ripe age of nineteen. Never even got to enjoy a decent hangover.

This was only my second time in the Blue Room. Tactlessly called that for the blue paint slathered along the dirty walls. Tonight, I tried to keep a low profile. Unfortunately, low profile and reputation do not go well together. Don't get me wrong--I had a bright, shiny, diamond-plated reputation, and that was how I liked it. That was the way I had made it this far in life.

I straightened my shoulders again and walked toward the back to lean against the wall. On the lookout for scum. What's scum you may ask? Scum is what I call the bad guys. They are the reason for my studded reputation. The nasty, evil, undead that roam through the world side-by-side with humans, causing mayhem and disasters. The ones that murder and rape and steal. Not all the undead are bad, but they definitely are not all good. Trust me, I'm not one of the good guys either, but I like to rid the world of the bad ones on a daily basis. Why? Well, what the hell else am I going to do while stuck in this ridiculous limbo of existence? How long am I stuck here? I couldn't tell you. Did I mention I am the only Forgotten that I know? That anyone I know, knows? Well, I am. At least I'm the only one to survive more than a week after the change. One of a kind, you could say. Unique. Guess no one else could handle the heat. Or rather, the horrors?

I leaned against the back wall, propped one black boot up against the wood and leaned my head back. It had been a long day, but I was too restless to go home. I hadn't been able to sleep last night, tossing and turning until dawn, then I had taken a very long ride to exhaust myself and ended up here. I could have easily fallen asleep now if my brain would shut up. That was one of the reasons I had that hard earned rep, to drown out the images and memories that my brain was constantly providing for me. And no, I'm not some crazed vigilante out kicking ass for revenge. I was a social outcast I suppose. The angels of both light and dark wanted me in their ranks so much to the point that they were constantly trying to kidnap, torture or seduce me. Whichever came easiest to them. There were very few that I actually trusted with my life. Others, I wouldn't be stupid enough to turn my back on them.

Like I said, I was a wanted woman. Why? Not quite sure. After spending the first year of my new life running and hiding, I spent the next two years basically being a badass bitch that didn't give two shits about anything except alcohol and sex. It wasn't so bad until I woke up from one wild night in bed with a vamp. Not my best day. Not his either when he tried to stick his teeth in my neck. Needless to say, he didn't call me back for a second date.

Now, I rid the world of any scumbags that cross my path, or just piss me off. So, in the last five or so years I started making a name for myself. Several names actually. Only those that I trust, know my true name is Crimson. The rest of the world seemed content to make up their own. I have started a list in the passing years. There was Blood Bitch, Slayer, Forgotten, Red, Titanium Angel, Titan..."smoking-hot-definitely-not-human-but-who-gives-a-shit-badass-babe over there against the wall."

Well, that was a new one. I tilt my head slightly in the direction of the whisper that I was not supposed to hear but did anyway. A group of guys sat at a table where they all had suddenly turned their heads in my direction. I watched from beneath my eyelids as their eyes widened and a few mouths dropped a bit. I knew what I looked like. Dark streams of wavy smooth hair, bright full red lips, big, smoky violet eyes paired with a black leather get up, a decent face and figure, and I was by horny male definition, "hot." I had aged little since my change, but luckily I had been mostly grown into my adult body at age nineteen. After the change, I had noticed very small differences, but nothing drastic through the years. Angels either aged so slowly that a year was the equivalent of a day or not at all. The Forgotten, a kind of messed up race; well, no one else had lived this long to have any idea what my life was going to be like. So, at this point, me being here at all, was a step ahead.

"Daa-ammmmn." One of them, a brunette male with sunglasses on his head nodded appreciatively in my direction. "Chase, my man if you are not interested in that, there is something wrong with you. One night stand or not, that chick is fi-ine."

I turned my head in their direction, forcing most of them to slam their attention anywhere but at me.

Only three continued to unashamedly study me. Sunglasses smiled at me while slowly undressing me from head to toe with his eyes. He irritated me and I ignored him. The light haired guy that had dubbed me a new name to add to my list peeled his eyes from my face and whispered to the man next to him. "Chase?"

I found the one they called Chase and did my own studying. From what I could see in the midst of a circle of buddies, Chase was what my horny female definition of "hot" was, to a T. A nicely toned, but not rock hard, upper body, dressed in black and rocking a leather vest, Mr. Chase was a pin-up Rockstar man. Sharp angular face with soft lips and white teeth. His hair was a straight jet black mess atop his head with sea blue eyes that just happened to sail across the room and latch onto mine. Shit. My heart actually stalled and slammed back into motion racing against my chest. My stomach fluttered and the alcohol in my system suddenly warmed me all over. I slammed a lid down on my reaction and sent a sweet but sexy smile over that way. His hand reached up and I watched as he unconsciously traced his lips with a finger, still watching my eyes. For the first time in a long time, I felt my insides gush and I turned away. No time for games, girl. Well, that was a total lie. I had a lot of damn time. I shook my head silently, no time for human games. Humans complicated shit, and the last thing I needed was problems. I focused my attention on the dance floor. Damn, I was all kinds of shook up. By a damn human. I felt like a high school girl again. I was hot and uncomfortable in my own skin.

I needed to pull myself together. I dug deep and pulled my nightmares from my memories, needing only a second, and I would be myself again. Images quickly flashed and emotions heightened. Coldness swept through me and iced over my slowing heartbeat. I regained control and masked any unwanted emotions. I took a deep breath and suddenly inhaled a vile smell. A mix of burnt flesh and hot blood, covered by a flowery perfume. Demon. Nice. I held my breath to keep the stench from burning my nose anymore and quickly searched the room. It was a she. Surprising, but not unheard of. She walked in dressed like a hooker with high heels and a dress that barely covered all the essentials. She dripped sex and drugs, as most demons did, attracting all the eyes in the room directly to her. Disgusting. I liked to think that there were three kinds of demons. First, the ones that hid the demon inside them, rejected it, and lived as human. Second, the ones that fell apart on the inside but had complete control on the outside. They were the ones that basically lived high --money, sex, and drugs being essential to them. The third and most dangerous were the ones that fell apart completely. They had nothing holding them together and, as a result, were ugly and grotesque, both inside and out. They cared about nothing and no one, and did nothing but create mayhem. Our winner here tonight was in the second group. She looked like the high roller for the street corner, but inside she was more than likely a scared little demon, trying to figure out what the hell she was doing. I rolled my eyes as all the humans continued to stare.

Did I mention that this was normal? That in this day and age humans knew about us, knew that we were everywhere, and were expected to be ok with it? No? Well, nowadays, the undead were taught about in high school. We were just another bunch of races to mix into the already diverse universe. It wasn't a peaceful coexistence, but no human was willing to start a war with the undead. After all, we weren't all bad. Especially since the good guys helped the humans along to good places when they died. Curious, I glanced back to the table with Chase and his friends. While his friends were clearly taking their fill from the demon ho, one set of watery eyes locked back onto mine. Damn it. I keep doing this to myself. I heard another person enter the bar but couldn't pull my eyes away. Conversations slowly restarted as the music picked back up. He blinked and broke the connection, I looked around. Demon girl went to the bar trying to swindle a drink from the bartender. Told him she was supposed to meet some guy named Joe. Dancing continued when the band returned the fast beat and the drinks started going around again. It was the time of night when they started to go down faster. I was debating my sanity about considering how to give this Chase guy some kind of hint that I might be interested when I heard my name across the room. Well, one of them.

"Titan."

It wasn't the long time no see, happy to finally meet again voice of a friendly. No it was the reverberating hiss of a vamp. The room once more stilled and quieted. I sighed, even the music halted once more. I slowly turned toward the voice. It was a rather large vamp too. And he looked pissed. Crap. I was just starting to wind down too.

He had the body of a linebacker and the scarred and abused face of a junkie. I scanned through my memories trying to place him as possible friend or enemy. I could not place him. So I planted both feet on the floor, plastered my official "I might look sweet but don't fuck with me" smile on and waited.

He crossed the room, the floor slightly shaking as he stepped. "Titan Bitch."

Oh damn, mixing it up now are we. I waited until he was right in front of me and continued to smile.

"Yes," I replied several tones lighter than his voice. "You seem to know me, but I honestly do not recall you." I may or may not have grinned and asked, "Did I stake a friend of yours?"

His eyes burned. "I don't have friends, but I know who you are and I know the boss will be thrilled to find that you snaked your way in. He has been looking forward to meeting you. Come with me now, and I will introduce you."

I smiled at the demand. "Actually I walked through the front door, no slithering involved. I really don't think I'm up for making friends tonight, thanks."

14

He darkened and leaned over me barring his teeth. "It was not a request."

I stood taller widening my stance and broadening my shoulders. This bloodsucker didn't scare me. No one did. "I'm afraid I must decline the invitation, you see, I have issues with authority. Could be the reason for my upstanding reputation." I winked. My reputation included the staking and decapitating of several vamps. "Tell your boss that I'll catch him another day." I got closer. "Now back the shit off," I whispered.

"He will not be pleased, Ice Queen."

I rolled my eyes--did this guy come up with these in his sleep? He stood and took a small step back. I relaxed the tiniest bit thinking how bad that could have gotten and it was enough for him to get the jump on me. He slammed me into the wall pinning me by the neck. He squeezed, but I just laughed. I felt my neck bruising and the bones slowly splintering. People all around us either froze with shock or took off not wanting to be in the midst of a fight. He smiled, his sharp teeth glistening with saliva and he punched me in the gut with his other fist. It felt like an elephant had just charged into my stomach sending all that wonderful whiskey burning back up my throat. I swallowed it back down while the room pitched forward for a second but turned back upright just as fast. Well, there goes a rib or two. Damn these vamps were strong. Especially this guy. He tightened his grip on my throat and I started to see a black fog creep into the edges of my vision as oxygen was depleted, but still I smiled at him. Well, passing out would be a bit embarrassing, plus who knows where I might wake up this time. I was thinking of my best way out of this when he suddenly paused.

It was the demon that stopped him. With a little hissy fit. If I could have rolled my eyes without passing out, I would have. The girl marched right up beside him and whined.

"Now, Billy, I came all the way over here because Joe asked me to, and if I do not see him in the next two minutes, I am taking my sweet self-home, and you can tell him that I do not like to be kept waiting." Her eyes bore into him and he looked away from her. No, I wasn't fond of staring into the madness of a demon's glare either.

Billy the vamp lessened his grip on my neck slightly. He looked back at me clearly torn between which one of us was more important. The demon ho that obviously had an important meeting with the boss or the Titanium Angel. I wasn't going to point out who was clearly more important, that was his job after all. Besides, I didn't think it would help my situation at all. I didn't have time to wait for his answer. I slammed my hand back against the wall into the decrepit fire alarm, crossing my fingers that it was up to code. It started screeching and sprinklers let loose above our heads. People screamed and stampeded out the door.

Billy stood frozen not sure if what had just happened actually happened while the chick freaked out screaming and running in circles. He looked at me with red angry eyes and growled. I wiggled out of his grip, but he grabbed my hand and squeezed, pulverizing the bones. I held my breath not letting him hear me scream or cry out. My vision blurred and I heard a strong deep voice yelling from upstairs. Billy jumped and spun around toward the voice releasing me. Must be Joe. I bolted into the rest of the crowd merging with them until I was outside in the cool dark night. I leaned up against the next building in the black shadows and tried to catch my breath. Broken hand, broken ribs, and more than likely some damage to my neck. I spent ten minutes trying to think about where I had parked my ride when I realized that there was no way I could drive it. And I could drive under some hard circumstances, but with one hand out of commission for the night and broken ribs I was already pushing iffy. My vision was still swaying, which told me that I definitely was not driving. Great. I stood back up and tried to steadily walk down the sidewalk. I made it about four doors down, right outside a small diner before my knees started to shake. I shoved into the diner and plopped down into the first available booth. It was quiet, but no one seemed to take notice of me. I glanced around real quick only seeing a few tables occupied. Good. The waitress scooted over, took one look at me and raised a brow.

"Honey, you look like you got in a fight with a mountain lion and just barely escaped with your life."

I smiled up at her. "Close."

Her green eyes sparkled. "Whatcha need, dearie?"

"Bowl of ice, a towel and one hot chocolate filled with the good stuff."

"You got it." She smiled and walked away.

I closed my eyes and rested my forehead on my good hand. What I really needed was my bed. But in order to get home, I needed two hands and full vision. A bowl of ice was set before me with a red kitchen towel. I barely lifted my head. Just shoved my broken hand into the ice and held my breath.

I heard her talking to the other table, "Food will be out in a minute guys."

She shuffled over to me and I slit open my eyes to watch her set a hot chocolate brimming with marshmallows and whip cream before me. I hate coffee. So this was the next best thing to get my ass moving.

"One hot cocoa filled with the goo... Oh my, God look at your hand!"

Crap.

"Honey you need to hightail yourself to a hospital right now!"

I shook my head and looked up at her. "No, I am all right, it's just a little bruise."

She shook her head and studied me then her gaze fell to my throat. She squealed loud enough to have eyes turning my way. "You have bruises the size of Texas on your neck young lady," she bent forward and whispered to me with worry. "You tell me right now, are you in trouble?"

I smiled warmly up at her. "Trouble is my middle name."

She huffed and straightened her back as a bell rung from the back. "Well, you be careful, you hear? Before RIP is stuck in there too."

I chuckled at the humor. Been there, done that. She hustled away muttering about stupid abusive men. How cute, she thought a man was beating me up.

I chugged half my cocoa as my eyes started to focus again. She brought out a tray loaded with food and I heard a deep but quiet voice and for some reason it gave me a shiver up my spine. Strange. I shrugged it off my already overloaded plate of things to deal with and chugged the remainder of the cup licking the whip cream off my lips. I put my head back down and left my hand in the ice for another ten minutes. I studied it when the ice started to melt. The swelling had at least slowed and my super awesomeness was already starting to heal the bones. I flexed my fingers, but they just crackled and shot pains through my arm. Damn, not quite there, Crim. I needed to get home and deal with this later. I dried off my hand and left more than enough money on the table. I had liked the lady. I stood and made my way through the diner to the restroom in the back. I passed the table full of guys that were just finishing what looked like burgers and fries. The three that were facing me looked vaguely familiar, but my tired brain pushed them aside and I wobbled past. I'm sure I looked a fright. Tangled damp hair, dark tired eyes, broken mangled hand, bruised neck and holding my side like it was going to fall out. I confirmed this when I pushed into the run-down restroom and took a good look in the mirror. Oh yeah, I was rocking the dead and creepy look. I did my best to freshen up and attract less attention, but it was what it was. Taking a deep breath, I pulled open the door and cradled my bad hand against my chest. The other hand went immediately to my ribs to make them feel a little more secure. When I stepped through the doorway my worn down self instantly went on alert. Red alert. Red hot boiling alert. A shadow leaned casually against the opposite wall waiting for me.

Sure enough the human from the bar with mesmerizing blue eyes stood there watching me. Chase.

I froze, not sure what he wanted or if he was waiting for someone else. My eyes found his and once again they held. After thirty seconds of awkward silence, I broke away from his intense stare and found the rest of his friends watching me from the table. My back straightened. No time for bull shit. I started to step away, but when he spoke my legs froze and I slowly twisted back around.

"Are you alright?" He asked with a deep English accent that sounded fully concerned.

My heart sped up as my body reacted to his stare and his voice.

"Fine," I whispered breathlessly. "Thanks." I turned back away, took one step and stumbled as a knee buckled.

A hand grasped my arm firmly breaking my fall. My vision started to blur again. Another hand touched my hip, gently shoving me back against the wall for support.

"Let me help you." He whispered close to my ear still holding onto me with both hands. Probably afraid I would pitch over at any second. Definitely a possibility.

"Sorry kid," I leaned my head back against the wall pushing away the dizziness. I slanted my eyes open, "unless you can drive a motorcycle you can't really help me right now."

"I can." He was extremely close now and I wasn't sure if it was him getting closer or me starting to fall into him.

"No, you can't help..." I broke off suddenly, forgetting what he couldn't do because his face was close enough that I could smell the root beer on his breath. His eyes were breathtaking up close. Bright and dark swirls of green and blue. His hand still rested firmly on my hip against my bare skin where a burning heat started to build. Then I started thinking of all the things that he could do to help me out. I flushed when I felt myself purr like a cat. I started to walk again trying to escape the bad situation, but my legs were not interested. Both knees buckled and I fell fast. Well, I would have fallen fast if Mr. Hot Stuff hadn't scooped me up like a child and settled me into his arms. His very warm and comfortable arms. I closed my eyes while the room spun.

"Where...."

I popped open my eyes, quite certain I had heard him talk.

He watched me for a second. "Your bike, where is it?"

I closed my eyes again and whispered, "Fifth and Main," before the darkness closed in.

Chapter 2

I'm ashamed to admit I do not remember much after that. Bits and pieces really. Being carried and tightly held against a stranger's chest through the dark streets. Arms and legs caging me in front of him while he zoomed through the darkness. Then a warm blanket and a soft bed. Gentle hands. Then nothing.

I slit open my eyes knowing from the smell that I am not home. The room is dark. Blinds are pulled shut blocking sunlight and the door to exit the room is slightly ajar. I am in a bed, fully clothed (yes, I checked), minus boots and jacket. The bed is wooden, a brown so dark it looks black wood, with white sheets and a bright blood red comforter. A glass sits on the matching nightstand with water. I reach for it and find that my hand has been wrapped up. A part of me is touched, the other laughs at the wasted effort. Someone took care of me, cute but wasted time. I chug the water (yes, just water). I checked that, too. In my life, water offered is never just water. It is poison, sedative, drugs, or even potions. I slowly get to my feet and after I find them steady, I slowly walk to the door. I watch every corner and every space for movement as I walk. You never know who could be hiding in the shadows. Following a hallway out into a living area that is just as dark, I find the human fast asleep on a couch. I instantly like him a bit more when I see my prized bike sitting beside the door, inside his apartment. Good boy.

There is a window and curious to know where I might be, I pad over to it and quietly shift the blind just enough for me to see out. Afternoon sun strokes my cheek and I squint, stepping closer. Imagine my surprise to see us several floors up in an apartment building. I looked down at the busy city street and turned back around to see if my bike was really inside this kid's living room or if I had imagined it. Sure enough, it sat there.

"Elevator." He whispered hoarsely from the couch.

I didn't jump, a lot. But sure enough my blood started to boil. He sat up and swung two bare feet onto the gray carpet. Black pajama pants and cotton T-shirt stretched across his body. I watched like a starving puppy as he rubbed his eyes and face then ran a hand through his disheveled locks. My stomach fluttered. "Elevator?" My voice might have come out a little hoarse, but I was a badass, it was expected.

He fixed those eyes on me and did a slow head to toe inspection. My badass flew out the door replaced by the horny female in desperate need of special attention. "I snuck the bike up through the elevator. No one was around. I figured you might skin me alive if I left it down in the lot overnight."

24

I looked at his face. He was very serious. I felt a corner of my mouth twist upward.

"Good choice."

It was quiet for a moment. Awkward. I cleared my throat and put my hand in my back pocket cradling the other against my chest. He watched me. "Well, this an interesting 'morning after'." Crap, did I say that out loud?

"I'm actually surprised that you're still here." He studied me. "You strike me as the 'sneak out in the morning light and never hear from you again' type.

"Guilty," I smiled wickedly. "But I would not have left my bike."

"Of course." He watched me for another moment, before standing and slowly walking toward me.

My heart flung into action while my eyes watched him move closer.

"Let me see your hand." He stopped so close that I could feel the heat radiating from him against my skin. I still had my hand cradled against my chest and didn't move, just watched him warily. He slowly reached and wrapped a hand around my wrist brushing my chest. He pulled it toward him and gently unwrapped it. I stood frozen, amazed at my bodies' reaction to this human. He spread my fingers out and held it up between us. Squinting in the darkness he stepped

25

forward and reached behind me to release the blind. Our bodies brushed and zings of electricity raced through me. When he stepped back the sunlight fell freely through the window behind me onto him. Butterflies. Really? I huffed at my obvious problem today with keeping my emotions under control. He grabbed my elbows and spun so that I was now in the sunlight and he in the shadow. He once again spread out my hand and studied it gently probing. The bones were nearly healed, it was just angry red and black with bruises. "Much better." He then raised his eyes to my throat and gently tipped my chin back and side to side. "Also better." He released me and slowly reached down to my ribs. I held my breath as his fingertips feather touched my side. He stooped down in front of me and gently lifted my shirt up to show my rib cage. As soon as his fingertips brushed on my bare skin along the broken rib bone, I sucked in a breath and slammed my eyes closed. He froze. Shit. I really needed to get myself under control. Acting like a horny virgin because a hottie human was rubbing my belly. Sheesh, Crim put a lid on it.

"Not better?" He whispered. I opened my eyes. His face was full of concern. Oh good, he thought that when he touched it, it hurt. Good, I can work with that.

"Guess not," I whispered through clenched teeth.

"If they are not healing like the bones in your hand, you should probably go back to bed."

"Uh huh," I stepped away and walked around the room looking anywhere but at him. "Are you some kind of Doctor?"

I heard him stand and slowly walk toward the kitchen. "My parents are both in the field, I am not. But I know a thing or two about broken bones." I watched him go in and pull open the refrigerator. "Hungry?"

I shrugged. I felt kind of strange accepting so much help from the human. Now, he wanted to feed me too. As if on cue, my stomach growled.

He raised a brow. I shrugged again and continued my study of his place. A lot of gray and black and every once in a while something bright and colorful. Grey carpet, black couches, and royal blue lamp shades? I shook my head.

"So what do you do, Chase?" I drawled out the name. It was the first time I had actually used it. He paused for only a second before returning to making food. I also noticed the balcony between the kitchen and living room. My brain made a mental note. Easy escape, or easy access.

"I'm a photographer."

"Hmmmm." That explains the large photos that were randomly hung on empty walls. I looked at one that was above the couch, a landscape view of the city at dusk. Nice. Also explained the expensive looking camera sitting on the countertop.

"What about you," he paused. "I don't even know your name."

"Does it matter?" Melting cheese and butter drifted over my way and my legs made an involuntary beeline toward the kitchen. He was frying up some grilled cheese sandwiches. My stomach clenched in hunger. They happened to be one of my favorites. I sat on the barstool across from him at the counter and watched him work.

"Well, I carried you after you fainted, drove your bike home with you in tow, brought your bike into my living room, tucked you into my bed, took care of your injuries and now I'm making you 'morning after' breakfast. I think that deserves at the very least a name."

"I did not faint. I fell asleep, very rapidly." I defended myself, I did not need rumors flying that I fainted. That would considerably dent my hard earned rep. "I'm sure you rather enjoyed driving my bike, and just so you are aware, no one else in the entire universe has been given that privilege. I'm also sure you found some kind of pleasure in tucking me in and attending my boo-boos just like you are enjoying my company right now while you make food." I raised my brow and dared him to argue.

He didn't argue, just looked at me with a dead serious expression. "Name?"

"Hmmmm, there are so many it's hard to pick just one."

"The real one would be nice."

I pretended not to hear him. "There's Bitch, Ice Queen, Slayer, Red, Lost One..." He put down what he was holding and put both hands on the countertop, leaning over me while I continued. "Forgotten, Bloody Bombshell, Candy Cane, Titanium Angel, Titan for short..."

He sighed with exasperation. "Why do you not just tell me your true name?"

I looked him dead in the eyes. "There is a great deal of power in a name. Less than five people on this earth know my true name, Kid." Actually, I only knew one person that had that knowledge, and he was hidden away in the mountains.

"My name is Chase, not Kid." His eyes crackled as he pushed this point. I shrugged, and he slid a plate in my direction. "And if you don't trust me enough to give me your real name, then what shall I call you? I'm not using any of those ridiculous things."

I shrugged once more as he sat across from me at the kitchen bar. He had made me two very good looking sandwiches and my mouth started to water. He picked up his and started to eat so I picked up my own. It tasted just as good as it had looked, and considering he had done so much to help me out I gave up thinking he had the guts to poison me now. He finished his first and sat back to watch me finish mine.

"So if you won't tell me who you are, are you at least going to tell me what you are?"

I rolled my eyes, "I have no idea what you are talking about I'm just an everyday sweet angelic little lady."

He leaned toward me once more and irritation sparkled in his eyes. "Cute."

He started listing. "Extremely hot, light as a feather, but packed with muscle, pain resistant and rapid healing abilities," he paused for a second then continued. "Obviously amazing hearing, lots and lots of enemies, very few friends, and will not give me your true name." He paused again. "Did I miss anything?"

I smiled. "Extreme badass, biker chick, loves food, cats, Christmas music, sex, and sunshine."

His lips twitched up into a smile. "Christmas music?"

I rolled my eyes. Most normal guys would latch onto the sex part. "Shut up."

His grin stretched wide.

I huffed and stood up. I grabbed his empty plate and mine and marched over to the sink.

He cleaned up while I scrubbed. "Ok. You like food and sunshine and did not try feasting on my blood last night, so I can cross off vampire."

"Slimy creeps."

"You're not red-eyed and foaming at the mouth with insanity, nor are you walking around like you own the world demanding money and sex, so I can rule out Demon."

"Who said anything about not wanting money and sex?" I asked incredulous while rinsing the plates and setting them in the rack to dry. This kid was cracking up my mysterious persona in a matter of minutes. "There was a time in my life that that was what I lived for."

He paused. "Well, that explains the enemies vs. the friends."

I froze surprised and offended, even though it was totally true. I slowly dried my hands and laid the towel back down. "Listen here Kid, thanks for the help but do not presume that you know anything about me..."

My words died in my throat when he suddenly grabbed me and spun me around toward him. He then backed me into the counter caging me in with his arms. My breath froze in my lungs when his warm hard body pressed against mine and his face got so close that I could see every speck of color in his eyes.

Every nerve in my body started going haywire. And for once, I could not think of anything to say.

Anger sparked and rolled off of him in waves. "My name," he stated very clearly, "is Chase." His head bent lower and his lips were only a breath away from mine. "I know nothing about you because you play games and avoid giving me true answers. So, Angel," he drawled out the name making a shiver race up my spine. "If I make any presumptions, it is only because I give a fuck about you and have no other information to go by."

I stared up at him still frozen with shock. He cared about me? He didn't even know me. That obviously had not mattered though. He has taken care of me, a complete stranger. Took me home, cared for me, heck even cared about my bike. When was the last time I could honestly say someone gave a shit about me? Usually the D-bags I had the pleasure of running into only cared about destroying me or turning me into their right hand. Wanted woman, remember? To have someone actually care about me, just me... it was breathtaking. I was still at a loss for words, and I lost track of the conversation. I watched the swirling heat in his eyes and felt my body heat up until I was swirling around with him. He wants a name, idiot.

So me, lost in the moment of insanity, whispered while staring up into those memorizing eyes, "My name is Crimson, I am a Forgotten."

He paused processing what I had said and his eyes found my lips. His hand reached up and touched my cheek. "Crimson," he whispered drawling it out and making me shiver. "How could any sane person forget you?"

I had no answer, no time to give him one. His hand slid back along my throat pulling me closer and his lips found mine making everything erupt into flames.

Our bodies pulled together like magnets and his hand fisted into my hair. The force of passion made my stomach flip and heat pool inside me like melting butter. My arms stretched up and wrapped around his neck while his tongue dived into my mouth and I tasted the salty butter on him. Flame stretched from my belly and outward and I felt my back tingle. He shoved me harder up against the counter and his other hand slid down along the curve of my bottom and he squeezed. I started to purr like a cat in wild madness. My chest was smashed up against his firm one and I felt my nipples start to harden against him. He pushed against me trying to get closer, while I pulled at him wanting the same thing. His leg fell between mine and his thigh pushed up against the center of me. Fireworks exploded and I gasped out loud my head falling back while my eyes lost focus. His lips traveled down my throat while he pushed his leg against me again. I moaned and he tilted my head back down pulling my lips back to him. The kiss lasted forever. It was a wild rush that never ended. An adrenaline spike that never stopped. It had to have been hours that we stood with our mouths and bodies fused together in heat. My soul stretched outward wanting to keep whatever was making me feel so amazing. It had been a very long time since anyone had kissed me like this. Since anyone had kissed me just to kiss me. In my rebellious years kissing had just been a short prelude to sex. Not pure passion unleashed in flames and heat. This was different, it was new. I started to shake. My entire body trembled like a leaf in a harsh wind. He noticed and pulled back to look at my face. His lips were swollen and red, but he kept his hands in my hair and around my waist. He studied me as my body trembled against its will, and I smiled. "You wanted answers, here is one for you." I closed my eyes and let my wings free. They snapped away from my back like a rubber band, softly and gracefully filling up the space behind and around me. He stared, at first in shock, then in amazement, then in yearning. When they were fully expanded and the weight sat comfortably where it belonged, I sighed. My wings only threatened to come out on their own when I was extremely emotional. Apparently, I had let this guy get me all wound up. He still held me tightly against his body, not seemingly at all deterred by the sudden change in me. His lips found mine again, but this time they were soft and gentle. Slow and exploring. I sighed and melted against him.

This was probably a bad idea. Human interaction wasn't smart. Human relationships... really bad idea. Undead and humans could live somewhat peacefully side by side, but relationships never quite worked out.

First, we were stronger, if for whatever reason we lost control; well, things got broken. Another thing, obviously humans were mortal, they would eventually die. Things get dangerous around me. A human could become deadweight or even leverage. I was not ready to lose someone I cared about again. If humans and one of my kind got together, both usually fell off the grid. Why? Survival.

I stiffened a little and slowly pulled my arms down from his neck. He pulled his lips from mine and rested his forehead against me while we both caught our breath. His hands moved toward my waist and settled on my hips. The sensation made my wings twitch. They ran from my shoulder blades down to the floor where they softly dragged behind when I walked. They curled toward him while he held onto me. Figures, even my wings like him. Suddenly too warm I took a step to the side breaking our close contact. The feathery tips curled farther toward him reluctant to let him go.

He reached down and lightly stroked one from my hip to the tip. The sensation was like a stroke down my spine and if he would not have spoken I might have melted into a puddle on the floor.

"Why are they red?" He whispered hoarsely. "I have only ever seen white or black, never half white and red." His eyes moved up to mine just in time to see my reaction.

I turned cold as the pain overwhelmed me and felt a sudden need for distance. "Blood stains."

I backed away suddenly and turned. I heard him inhale sharply as what I said processed and he got a full view of just what I meant. I felt his warm eyes travel from my head and down. Bright white wings rose over my shoulders and fell gracefully to the floor like a bright beautiful cape. It would have been angelic if not for the deep red blood stains that had soaked from the bottom tips up to my thighs. It had been almost a decade and still the blood stained the delicate feathers like it was yesterday. I shivered. My heart started to beat too fast. I needed to go. I flexed my hand and felt only a tense pull. I spotted my boots by the door and had them on in a second. My jacket hung on a rack and I grabbed it. I swung around and walked toward my bike. He watched me, saying nothing. My hands started to sweat, but I needed to leave. Now. I straightened my shoulders and plastered my badass smile on. It was a bitch move, but I didn't care. Coldness was the only thing I had to give. I stuffed my jacket into the saddle bag and zipped it up. "Thanks for helping me out, I'd love to stay and chat, but I got places to be."

He just watched me for a moment with an impassive expression. This was what he had said that he expected anyway, right? Well, I was never one to disappoint. "Yeah." He crossed his arms over his chest in a defensive stance. "See you around I guess."

I winked and kicked up the kickstand. I pushed my bike toward the balcony.

"Uh, the elevator is that way." He pointed behind him.

"Uh huh." I shoved open the glass doors and pushed my bike out into the warm sunshine. I swung my leg over and sat on the soft leather seat with a sigh. The sun warmed my cheeks and I took a deep breath, closed my eyes and tilted my head back to enjoy it for a moment. My wings spread out wide also loving the warmth. It was a moment of pure relaxation. I heard a whine and click and my mouth twitched into a sly smile. I cracked open my eyes and tilted my head toward him. He snapped another picture and I raised a brow.

"Just in case," he said with a shrug.

I nodded and bit my lip. It was good that he was taking this so well. My wings started twitching toward him so I kickstarted the bike. It roared to life beneath me and I smiled. I couldn't help myself and I looked back to him once more. He stood leaning against the doorjamb, camera in hand quietly watching me with those mesmerizing blue eyes.

"See you around, Kid." I heard another click and I shook my head. I stretched my wings out fully, wrapped my fingers around the handlebars and squeezed my thighs together putting my toes beneath the foot bars. I pushed down with my wings and pulled up with my hands giving it enough gas to pop a wheelie at the same time. The front end lifted above the balcony railing and my back tire squealed on the concrete pushing me forward. My wings flapped once more lifting me and bike over the rail and down over the edge. I only needed another flutter or two to guide me smoothly onto the street below. As soon as tire met pavement I tucked my wings away, cracked the throttle open wide and flew down the street away from the human. It was best, for the both of us if we never met again.

Chapter 3

For some reason, my body and brain do not like to agree on things. For example, my brain decided that a lot of alcohol would help me get through this evening. Now, my body was screaming its outrage at me. It had been three weeks now since I had left the human in my dust because my brain had told me it was the right thing to do. My body was pissed. My brain had informed me over and over that humans do not mix with angels, never-mind a Forgotten. My body had insisted that we had not had any problems getting along back in his apartment. My brain informed me that if I hung around him too much, I would likely get him killed. My body had scoffed at me and told me that anyone would have to go through it first. So you see what I have been listening to for the past three weeks? Not even counting the two cents my wings were adding to the mix. They shivered when I remembered him, they craved his fingers softly stroking them. They quivered at night when I dreamt of him. Very hot dreams. It was bad. I had it bad. For a human. For Chase.

So now I am standing in an alley, looking across the way at two demon D-bags that were clearly interested in beating me to a pulp. Usually, this was not an issue. I would have tussled with them a bit, and eventually disposed of them without breaking a sweat. Tonight was a different story. Tonight, I had specifically left my precious bike at home, so that I could go sit in a bar, mind my own business and get wickedly plastered. I had done all of those things until someone said he recognized me from some billboard and tried to talk me into his bed. As if I was some kinda pin-up poster girl that posed for a ridiculous billboard! He kept referring to me as Biker Angel. It kinda pissed me off because I had no clue what he was talking about and I may have punched the guy in the nuts when he started asking me if my wings were real or just a costume that I had put on.

Perhaps if I was not already into my second bottle of whiskey (yes, second bottle, I told you my intention for the evening), I may have noticed that this guy and his friend were not human. So after I punched him in the nuts, the owner made me finish my drink, pay my bill and he kicked me out. And of course, they followed me. Which gets me to right now. Me, trying with difficulty to stand straight while looking at two sex and drug poster boys that were very interested in ruining my fascinating complexion. I sighed and chuckled at my situation. Two-bottles-of-whiskey-down, two-bottles-of-whiskey, you take one down and pass...Sorry, I was having a moment. I shook my head to clear it, crouched a little to gain steady footing and went to work.

It might have been a good hour later that I was walking down a familiar street towards a familiar building. I had taken care of the demons, sloppily but dealt with, and even managed to snag a new bottle of alcohol from a liquor store. I wasn't quite sure what it was, but it tasted like apples and it was green. I liked it. So, I had chugged the first one and went back in for a second. The guy had hesitated in selling me the second, but I flashed him my cutesy smile and he had pushed right over. I also noticed that when I smiled he looked behind me to a magazine and back. Curious I turned my attention and found myself starring, at myself. I blinked and stepped closer. It was me sure enough. Me sitting on my bike in brilliant sunlight on a certain balcony. I was looking at the camera with a sexy smile and smoldering look.

The photo was in black and white so my wings were not red, which was interesting. They were fanned out completely as if stretching to collect the sunlight. I had two sudden thoughts at once: oh shit, I really was a pin-up poster girl, with a half second of regret for the two guys I just demolished and that human had not only shared a photo of me but was probably making a shit ton of money off of it. I mean shit, I looked good! So I turned my smile back on and mentioned something about doing underwear and motorcycle ads next to the guy, which certainly seemed to brighten his day and left with my new bottle. Now I was here on this street, about a third of the way through my second bottle of apple goodness and staring up at that window wondering if I had the balls to get myself into this situation. Of course, my brain was talking but I was not understanding it. The only thing I was understanding right now was a yearning for a stroke or two. A stroke down my wings, down my belly, or against my tongue. I shook my head. Well, I was here, might as well rip into him for making me a model and not asking permission first. I let loose my wings and sprung to the balcony. I slipped a little on the landing, but I was still silent. His apartment was not. It was lit up and quite noisy. I took another chug from my bottle and looked out toward the city. I almost dropped the damn thing. There, in the distance, but close enough that I had a perfect view was a billboard of me. This picture was in sepia, almost the same as the other except that my eyes were closed and my head tilted up toward the sun. I felt a small blush rise in my cheeks. (It happens when I drink too much.)

It looked like I was about to orgasm on my bike. I swallowed and tried to turn away. Each detail from the photo jumped out at me. My wings were white and a brownish color like antique gold. My expression was purely orgasmic and I radiated sex and heat. My body was tense and relaxed at the same instant, kind of a pain and pleasure feeling. I softly whistled. So maybe the guy had talent, but he had quite the material to work with.

When I heard voices inside, lots of male voices, I realized that this is what Chase got to look at every single day when he looked outside. It made me smile. Maybe I wasn't the only one that had suffered the last three weeks. My smile broadened. It sounded like I was missing a party, and I hate to miss parties. My wings fluttered as if remembering where they were but I tucked them into my back and I shimmied against the balcony door that was slightly ajar. I heard a tv, as well as video games, and what sounded like about ten males, all in various stages of drinking. Even in my inebriated state, I could hear the drawls and pitch changes in their voices. I slowly slid into the doorway in the darkness just enough to see inside. I was right at least nine guys that I could see. Some stood along the far wall looking at some photos, some sat on the couch watching tv and others sat on couches across the room playing video games on another tv. They all were in various stages of drinking, but all seemed to be talking about the exact same thing, me. I searched the room for that familiar body and found him sitting with his back to me on a barstool with a beer in his hand listening to the conversation. My body reacted instantly and I took another swig to dull it.

I recognized Sunglasses when he turned in our direction. "Dude, I cannot believe you let this one get away without even one fuck." He shook his head and glanced over his shoulder to the photos a few were still studying. "Shit son, I would have been all over that fine ass." He moved toward Chase and I was able to see what the photos were. I should have known they would be the originals. The color copies of those quick snaps he had taken. All very large photos of me as I rode (or flew) away and stomped on his ego. Poor guy. Chase was quiet, did not seem to have anything to say back to Sunglasses.

"Dude," he said to him quieter after sitting beside him. "Me, I would have done it while she was out cold."

The wind suddenly blew past me into the room and I saw Chase's shoulders stiffen. I stepped in. "Now that would not have been much fun for me, would it?"

The room stilled and every head whipped in my direction. Chase, very slowly spun on his stool with a slow sexy smile forming on those lips. Sunglasses whipped around in surprise and tried to recover his smooth attitude. Slime-ball. Glad it was Chase that had taken me home instead of that guy. I walked towards them and stooped down to whisper, "I would have murdered you in your sleep after cutting off your dick and shoving it down your throat." He choked on his beer and sputtered. I stood and winked at Chase before taking another chug from my bottle. No one moved. "Shit, you all look like you've seen a ghost or something." I chuckled at my own humor. They nervously twitched. "Ooookkkkaayy." I swung towards Chase. "Mind if I use your shower? I think I am wearing demon brains and…" I looked down at the black and red smears on my clothes, "…stuff." He smiled at me and nodded. I tipped my bottle to him took another chug, and walked through the room of tongue-tied people, down the short hallway and into the bathroom. I locked the door behind me.

Awkward! I stripped to my skin and half listened to the explosion of conversations in the other room. I drank another third of my bottle and waited until the water was hot. When it started steaming, I stepped in and moaned in appreciation. The water seared my flesh, but it felt so good that I simply stood for awhile letting it roll down my back. Let it run over my wings. They stretched out minimally in the tiny space, but the heat made them quiver and relax. I finally pushed myself to actually use soap, soap that was clearly male and it made my skin tingle. I reminded myself that I was very wasted.

I considered going right into his room and passing out, but then I remembered that I like parties and that tonight was about getting annihilated. I was having a little trouble remembering why I was getting annihilated, but it didn't bother me. I shut off the water and stepped out. Only one towel hung against the door so I used it to dry off. Next issue, nothing to put on. All I had was ick covered clothing. I considered them for a second, then threw them in the shower. I turned it on full blast until the room was packed with steam and hung them along the shower rod to dry. I wrapped the black towel around my torso under my arms and tucked it in. It covered me from chest to thigh, so I looked under the sink for something to brush my hair with. I found one tiny black comb and one extremely soft hairbrush. Neither would do me any justice so I just finger combed it and let it go. Heaven help the first person to see me in the morning, but drunk as I was, I guess I didn't care. I grabbed my bottle from the sink and flung open the door.

I found nine sets of eyes eagerly waiting in the other room. I smiled and cheered, toasting them with my bottle. Did I mention I was only wearing a bath towel? Again, too much alcohol. They all cheered back and lifted their drinks. I found Chase, sitting in the same spot watching me quietly with a small smile. "I'm borrowing some clothes." The smile turned into a grin and he lifted his beer and toasted me. I was glad I had been drinking, otherwise I might have told him to kick everyone out and meet me in the bedroom. I was still considering it, but my green bottle was against the idea. It wanted to party. I dug around in drawers and finally landed some black skinny jeans and a small black hoodie. No undies, but I was the only one that would know. I think. My brain had literally chosen that moment to stop working completely. I grabbed my bottle and padded barefoot back out into the living room. Conversations halted once more as everyone turned to me and I stopped. "Gawd, what do you people want?" I whined. I did my best happy girl smile and beamed, "Hi, I'm Titan. I like food and alcohol. I suck at video games but I can kick ass in real life and I came to party! Woohoo!" I raised my bottle and took another swig. There was only a second of hesitation before the others raised their beers and cheered back.

Conversations continued and I sighed in relief. I walked toward the kitchen to seek out some ice. I was feeling a heat wave coming on. I felt his eyes follow me and took another long pull from my bottle. It was feeling much lighter than I recalled and I frowned down at the little bit of green liquid. I must have been standing there for a good bit because he snuck up beside me without me noticing.

He grabbed the bottle, "Pucker. Interesting choice, Titan." He drawled out the name making a shiver travel up my treacherous body.

"I need more." I took it back and finished it off.

He studied me. "How many drinks have you had?"

I raised a brow. "A lot." I smiled at him and he swayed a bit.

"How many is a lot?" He watched me with a serious face.

"I dunno," I shrugged and pushed the button on the fridge door for some ice. "Like three or four." Two cubes fell out. I plopped one in my mouth like a lollipop and I put the other against my neck.

I looked up at him and he swayed again. "Not to worry, I'm good." I looked at him scolding, "But you, on the other hand, need to take a break. You can't even stand up straight." He looked at me in shock and confusion so I snagged the beer from in front of his lips and floated around him.

I heard him chuckle behind me and one of his friends comment, "that chick is wasted."

I shrugged it off and spotted an empty seat on the couch in front of the video games. I plopped down between two guys and crunched down on my ice cube. The other had already melted against my skin. They both paused and looked at me. "Ok boys, show me how it's done." I took a pull from Chase's beer and watched the tv. I felt them relax and then they both started talking to me about the game. The one on my left was the blonde kid from the bar that had given me my new name. He was called Brain, although I was pretty sure it was a nickname. On my right was Luke. He did not have too much to say but was nice enough. I tried to follow along with the game, but by the time my second beer was gone I was even more confused. So I just ended up cheering both players on with my wild screams and hollers. They both seemed to get a kick out of it, and eventually everyone sat around the tv watching them battle it out. They all cheered and yelled with me.

After my fourth beer, the conversation somehow switched to me again. Everyone started asking questions. I wasn't sure if they were actually curious or they just wanted to hear me talk like a drunken idiot, which was actually pretty funny. I was laughing at myself halfway through my sentences. It was just so funny. Someone asked me why I ride a bike when I can fly. I asked them why they drive a car when they can walk. Then I informed them that I enjoy a rumble between my legs. I couldn't keep a straight face and they all busted into laughter. Another kid asked me why I kill demons and such. I smiled sweetly at

Sunglasses (whom I refused to give the time of day by learning his real name) and told them, "Because they piss me off."

Even he laughed out loud for this.

By my tenth beer, I somehow ended up with a controller in my hand and was standing and yelling at the screen like it was the Super Bowl. They were now all sitting around cheering me on while I battled against Brain. Apparently he was the record holder here. Then after my defeat somebody managed to find skateboards. I have never skateboarded...sober. I found myself riding around the room making 'choo choo' noises and blowing the horn with my empty hand. The other held my beer of course. You think that's funny? You should have seen the line of five or six adult males that joined in behind me making a human skateboard train and chugging and choo-ing between drinks. It was so comical I am almost certain I laughed for ten minutes straight. Then they were concerned. I lay on the floor holding my stomach while I had just finished giggling uncontrollably. My mouth hurt from smiling so much.

Chase leaned over me. "Honey, I think you have had enough to drink. This is what, your thirteenth beer? I think you drank more than me."

I laughed. "Puh-leese! Afta my third bottle, it was smoooooth sailing." I made the gesture of sailing with my hand to prove my point. I laughed, but he suddenly looked serious.

"Third bottle? You told me you had three or four drinks."

I looked at him confused as to why this was a big deal. "Yeahhhh, three or fouurr bottless." I shrugged my shoulders. "Thasss wha I drink."

His eyes widened. "No wonder you can't stand up straight or talk in a full sentence." He shook his head. "You are going to regret this in the morning, Kid."

I huffed at the nickname that I used to use on him and he had turned into me. Rude! I raised my chin and crossed my arms. "No regrets, not human remember?" I winked and smiled. At least I think I did. I saw a shadow behind him. I was pretty certain it was Brain.

"Actually, angels are known for their phenomenal ability to tolerate alcohol, but after a certain amount, you would feel the effect just like us."

I cringed my nose in distaste. I suddenly was not a fan of Brain. I shushed him and tried to sit up. "Not normal angel." The room spun a bit but I closed my eyes so no one saw my weakness. I heard a few people stumbling towards the door as well as a few byes yelled in my direction. I waved in that direction and stayed where I was. When I opened my eyes I found Chase

50

standing at the door with Brain talking seriously. I concentrated.

"I have no idea how long she will be around this time. Might not see her for another month, or longer." He rubbed the back of his neck. "Not like I can just pick up the phone and call her."

"No." Brain looked at him in surprise. "You can do better. Didn't you know that after you learn an angel's name all you have to do is call it out loud and it is like a direct line to them?" Oh shit. "Like a beeper, only better. It lets them know you need them. That is one of the reasons angels are there when you die to guide you into the next life. People call out to them."

Chase stood in amazement. "I had no idea."

Brain smiled and looked back at me. I glared at him and the smile widened. "Good luck, Chase."

The door shut and I looked around the quiet room. It was actually already cleaned up. His friends must be the helpful kind instead of the leave dishes and garbage everywhere for the host to clean up friends. I closed my eyes as the room spun again.

After a moment, I felt him put his arms beneath me and pull me up. "Come on ya' drunken wench."

I moaned my disapproval at another lame nickname and the fact that he was making the room spin more. When I clearly no longer possessed the ability to walk he swung me up and carried me to his room. I might have moaned and groaned, but he just smiled and chuckled. He sat me on the bed.

"Sleeping in those?"

I shook my head. "Ol t-shirt. Cu-out back."

He disappeared for a moment and I heard the fabric ripping. He handed me the shirt with a chunk torn away in the back and walked out and into the bathroom. I struggled getting the hoodie over my head but managed to pull the T-shirt over my bare flesh without injury. I shimmied out of the pants feeling the cold night air on my skin and crawled up to the pillow. I crawled halfway under the soft blanket and lay on my stomach. I turned my head toward the center of the bed and let my wings out. They stretched out and fluttered once or twice before settling on top of and beside me in relaxation. I heard him come back in, but I couldn't fight my eyelids anymore. When the bed creaked beside me, I was falling fast.

Chapter 4

Everything spun. I mean everything. When my brain
started to pick its way back to the land of the living my
body dragged like a bag of bones. Everything felt
heavy and hurt. I moaned. My own brain seemed to
be swimming in a sea of confusion and dizziness. In
the distance I heard a chuckle. It made me angry, but
before I could say anything my head splintered and
cracked into a gazillion pieces. I moaned louder. That
chuckle came again, but louder this time. As my body
started to reconnect with my wayward mind, I slowly
became aware of my surroundings. First, there was a
possibility I was naked. I was not entirely sure, but
there was a lot of airflow on my skin. Second, I was
currently wrapped around a man. That, I was certain
about. My leg curled around a muscular leg, my arm
was wrapped around a rather snug and warm waist and
my head was nestled into a chest. It was a very nice
chest. Warm, smooth and soft but full of strength. Let
me tell you when I say I was wrapped around him, I
mean hanging on for dear life-tight. My leg was
holding on so tight that I could feel a decent package
bulging against my thigh. I moaned again and he
twitched. My wing had even taken full opportunity to
snag its way across his chest and the tip had snagged
around what felt like his ankle. Poor guy had no idea
what he was getting himself into. I attempted

movement starting with my fingertips. They brushed against skin and he tensed beneath me. I made the mistake of trying to open my eyes and when I did, everything exploded. My eyes burned and I hissed when my head splintered once more.

"Yeah, that might take a while." His hand that was currently wrapped around my waist moved to stroke my wings, while the other lightly combed through my hair.

The stroke of fingertips snapped my wings into attention causing them to quiver and flutter with need. I moaned again, but it started as a purr and ended painfully as the noise made my own head crack. I tried to raise my head from his chest and my eyes slitted open once more. The tiny amount of sunlight that filtered through the blinds seared my pupils. "Shit!" I dug my head back down into the warm darkness of his chest. I heard him chuckle again. I mumbled into his skin, "Laugh at me again and I will kill you." I had meant it to be threatening, but it came out sheepish and weak. His chest shook with muffled laughter. "I mean it. Move a muscle and I kill you."

He at least had the decency to whisper. "What happened to the 'no regrets cuz I'm not human" badass that was the life of the party last night?"

I moaned. "This never happens to me." I tried to lift my head a tiny bit. When it made the room spin but not splinter I slitted one eye open. It was unpleasant but not painful. "It's your fault."

His hands stilled. "Why is it my fault?" He asked incredulously.

"I was only drinking to get you outta my head." He froze. Shit, I have got to learn to filter the crap that comes out of my mouth.

His hand resumed stroking my wing while the other trailed from my head down my throat and along my arm. It snagged along a sleeve and I was grateful to see that I was wearing some sort of clothing. Scant as it was, it was something. Going by skin to skin contact it felt like it was at least covering half my chest and most of my lower essentials. My skin started to warm as my body started reacting completely uncaring how my brain felt. I needed to put some distance between us or I was going to start getting really-really close. "I need a shower." I slowly straightened my arms and pushed myself up. The room continued to spin. I closed my eyes for a minute not moving. When I opened them I found Chase sitting against the headboard with his hands behind his head watching me. His eyes sparkled with heat and laughter. "Enjoying the show?" My voice dripped with sarcasm.

He smiled as his gaze slowly roamed from my head to my knees. "Absolutely."

I followed his trail, my chest was nearly falling out of the shirt that had been ripped open for my wings, one sleeve down to my elbow and the other about to fall from my shoulder. The hem of the shirt just covered the apex of my thighs, but it was of course, white and left very little to the imagination. "What a mess," I groaned.

"You are definitely a hot mess." He stated matter of factually.

My wing reached out and gently closed his eyes. "Don't look."

I started to climb from the bed on shaky legs.

"Hell no, I'm sucking in every second before you take off again."

I bit my lip. That was what I was doing right?

I grabbed the pants and hoodie I had borrowed last night from the floor.

"You can throw your clothes in the wash if you want. I would have done it last night, but then you would have been able to leave without saying goodbye."

"Thinking things through are we?"

"Once burned," he smiled mischievously, "twice learned."

I trudged into the bathroom only shutting the door halfway. I was enjoying this guy. And we hadn't even had sex yet. A big deal for me, but...

Crap. My brain was already accepting it as a done deal. I pulled the clothes from last night out tossing them on the floor and turned the shower on full blast, letting the room heat up.

I tucked my wings in and pulled the shirt over my head. I added it to the pile and stepped in. The heat seared my skin and I moaned in pleasure. My wings stretched out a bit enjoying the heat. Some of the fogginess started to clear away and I heard and felt him come in the room. My muscles tensed and my heart picked up speed.

"So."

I waited. When he didn't continue, I offered, "So?"

"No bike in my living room today."

I smiled. "I don't take her out when I intend to get drunk, beat up, or otherwise impaired."

"So you planned on getting tanked last night."

"Certainly."

"Because of me."

I grinned. He was a smart one. Getting his answers while I was vulnerable.

"Getting to a point, huh?"

"Figured now was a good time."

"Why's that?"

"You're very naked and very hungover in my shower."

True. Decent hangover... Check. "Been naked and a lot worse before."

Without missing a beat, he replied. "I might also have some cinnamon rolls in the oven about to come out and be smothered in icing."

My mouth watered. Damn. This guy was good. I was about to come up with a smart ass remark, but my stomach chose that moment to grumble.

I could just imagine him smiling. The hot water ran hotter down my body and I swung my wing around to cover me while snapping the curtain open. He smiled while his eyes widened in surprise taking in every available detail.

"Are you bribing me?"

"Certainly," he winked.

I huffed and slapped the curtain back in place, and I heard him walk out chuckling.

I rinsed out my hair and shook out my wings.I used the fresh towel that had been placed on the counter for me and pulled his clothes back on. My pile of clothes was gone so I pulled the comb from under the sink and sat on the toilet to start the long process of de-knotting my head. I heard his feet padding along the carpet and smelt the cinnamon and sugar on him. When he propped himself against the door jamb I was about halfway up the tangle. He stood in his black pajama bottoms watching me for a minute then he grabbed the comb and my hand and pulled me into the living room. He sat me on the floor in front of the couch.

"Stay."

My eyebrows raised ready for an argument but when I saw him grab a plate from the counter my mouth glued shut.

He handed me the plate and sat behind me. I was too surprised to do anything. He pulled me back against him and started combing where I had left off. When a moment passed and I still had not moved, he grasped my shoulders and whispered next to my ear. "Eat."

My stomach, seemingly attuned to his demands, rumbled. His lips rubbed against my ear when they stretched into a smile. I huffed. I forced my body to relax against him and dug in. He had filled my plate to the brim with gooey goodness and I was instantly attuned to only the food. So it wasn't until I set the plate onto the coffee table and licked my fingertips that I noticed all of the tangles and knots were gone and he was just combing through over and over. It was slow and stroking and my wings perked up inside the hoodie in interest. I closed my eyes and tilted my head back. He set down the comb and shoved my smooth mass of hair over one shoulder. I felt his hands start to rub the back of my neck and my head hung forward to give him full access of my neck and shoulders.

It was quiet for a few minutes, then I felt the need to break the silence.

"Saw some interesting pictures on my way here last night."

"Did you?"

"Yes. Imagine my surprise to find myself on a magazine cover in a liquor store."

"Shocked were you?"

"More surprised to see myself on a billboard down the street."

"Saw that too, did you?"

"Hmmmm, interesting pictures."

"I rather thought so."

"I'm surprised you shared them with everyone instead of keeping them to yourself."

"That's the thing about photography, I can make the audience see only what I want them to see."

I looked over my shoulder and raised a brow at him, my curiosity toyed with.

He nodded to the far wall. "Go see for yourself."

I slowly stood and my wings relaxed against my back. As I walked they slowly tumbled down out of the hoodie and dragged along the carpet softly. He sat back on the couch watching me. I walked up close. On the wall arranged in a cluster were four different sized photos. I recognized the first as the one from the magazine cover. It was me sitting on the bike looking back at him with a sexy smile. This photo was in full color so the red on my wings stood out brightly against the golden sunshine. It was actually me. An angel, but different. A Forgotten. I was suddenly thankful that he had changed the coloring. It was bad enough I had people looking for me—I didn't need a trail leading them to my door. The next photo was the billboard snap. It was also in bright color. It did not look like I was getting the ride of my life while sitting on the bike. It actually looked like I was just taking in my freedom. Enjoying the sun. Taking it all in. My red tipped wings were stretched wide ready for flight.

I looked at the next two surprised. They were close ups of my face. Of my expression. The first he had snapped just as I had bitten my lip looking all uncertain about what I was doing. The second had been my genuine smile looking like I had no problems and I could conquer anything.

"Interesting."

"Isn't it?" He stood and slowly walked toward me. "Funny how a simple photo can catch such different emotions." He pointed to them one by one. "Sly, sure of yourself, enjoyment... Relaxation, freedom and taking it all in... Uncertainty, regret and troubled emotions... Happiness, optimism and love..."

I was stunned. He had taken so much from me, in just a matter of moments. I didn't know how to respond. Survival kicked in. If he could see these things, who else could?

"Are the ones that I saw the only ones you gave out?"

"Yes. I figured you would skin me alive if I showed the world first, who you are, and second, that under all that bullshit badass attitude that you have real emotions."

I sighed. "Good to know." I turned to walk away from the suddenly uncomfortable conversation.

"Why do you do it?" He asked me quietly as if afraid it might push me away.

I froze mid-step. "Do what?"

"Cover up who you really are. You act like you're untouchable, but you're not."

He came to stand in front of me. "You are breakable, just like everyone else. Why play it like you don't care?"

The air stilled around me. This was getting too deep. "I'm different." I couldn't continue to look in his eyes. So I walked away and stood by the window. Away from his eyes. "No one in the entire universe is like me. I am the only Forgotten to live."

"How?"

"None of the others survive."

"I don't understand."

My wings snap and pull into me with frustration. I start to shiver.

"When a human dies, an angel is supposed to be there to guide them along."

He shook his head, recalling his own knowledge. "Yes, to put them on a path. A path can lead anywhere. It can lead to being a vampire, demon, warlock, angel or even nothing. Depending on the death from what I understand. A rough death is usually guided by a dark angel while an easy and calm death is guided by an angel of light."

"Yes." I locked eyes with him. "Do you know what happens when the angels all forget you?" My voice is cold and full of long ago anger. "When you spend years fearing death like the childhood monster under your bed, with only the small comfort of knowledge that someone would be there to guide you at the end. And the fear you feel when no one shows up."

"I have never heard of an angel forgetting to be there." He whispers with confusion.

"Exactly." I spun back to the window. "It happens so rarely. Like a grain of sand that falls through the crack. A single life falls from existence. I was forgotten. When I died there was no one there to help me pick up the pieces. When they finally remembered me, it was too late, I had already become a Lost One."

He sat on the arm of the couch watching me. Any closer and he knew I might bolt. "How..."

My head snapped up. "Don't ask me how I died. As long as I breathe I will never tell anyone what happened to me that night." Memories swamped my vision and I cringed. "There is only one person in the entire universe that knows, and that is the way it will stay."

"What happened after?" He changed the direction, skipping over the horrors that were now fresh in my mind.

"When both sides realized that the other had missed me, they both raced to my side. It is almost a game to them. Get there first and see how many team members they can get." I snarl bitterly, then take a deep calming breath. "It stays pretty much balanced so that the fight between good and evil always continues."

I turned from the window and slowly paced the room. "When they got there, I was already turned. You see, a Forgotten has no hope. A Forgotten can become anything. The soul reaches out for guidance and finding none it splinters and cracks into several directions." I remembered those moments well. The pain, then the cold fear when no light guided me. The hollowness and regret. Wondering what I had possibly done so wrong. The confusion when I started to break apart and stretch into murkiness. I shook away the memory. "A Forgotten can be reborn as many things. One may become half demon and half vampire. As you might guess, mixing does not go well. It messes with the mind. Pulls them in too many directions. They go insane and eventually lead to self-destruction. Some commit suicide, others are so destructive to the frail universe that they are removed by higher powers before death can come naturally. In most cases, a Forgotten will perish into nothingness within a week of the change."

He watched me. He said nothing, just watched my face, held my eyes.

"On the rare occasion, and I am talking once every couple centuries, that a Forgotten is born, one of the angels must watch over them. They have to babysit them until they are removed, whether naturally or by force. To the world, a Forgotten is an abomination, a monster. Luckily, the two that were sent after me decided to argue about who would take responsibility for me. They actually got into a fight long enough for me to run."

His brow lifted. "The Light and the Dark Angels fought over who would watch you?"

I nodded.

"Why does the Darkness care? I would have thought the Darkness would enjoy seeing a Forgotten roam about."

I smiled halfheartedly. "They don't like what they fear."

He nodded. "So you ran."

"So I ran. I ran because my wings were new and fragile. They were foreign to me and caked in dried blood and useless. I ran because I was very much on the edge of insanity and it was the only thing that I could think to do."

It was quiet for a moment. "How long ago was that?"

"Almost ten years."

His brows raised in surprise. "And you are the only one that has survived this long?"

"Yes."

"How?"

"That is the golden question, isn't it? That's why I am still running. There are several groups of humans and undead alike that want nothing more than to discover the answer to that question."

"Why?"

"Think about it, Rockstar. There has to be a reason that I'm still here. There has to be a key to unlock the secrets. If they found that key, think of all the monsters they could create."

Memories continued to drift to the surface and my eyes burned in anger. I could see my words processing in his mind. His eyes met mine. "You're not a monster."

"You don't know me."

"I know a hell of a lot more than you're willing to admit." He walked towards me again. "Titanium Angel, fitting for a facade. Let me guess what they say about you. Stone heart, fearless, painless, bulletproof, unemotional, indestructible and you have absolutely nothing to lose." He stepped up to me and grabbed my face sternly in his hands, "And it's all bullshit."

I stared up at him. He was right of course, but I wasn't admitting it. "It's not all bullshit. I have nothing to lose. I have no one to care about and no one to care about me." My voice is strong but I lose heat and it wavers. "I have nothing to fear because I have nothing to lose."Not anymore.

He pulled my face close as I felt a tear escape and run down my cheek.

"You could lose yourself, you could lose Crimson."

"She is already lost," I whisper. "Has been for a very long time."

He watches my face. "Then maybe we should find her." Watching my eyes, he lowers his lips and gently kisses me.

It was gentle, sweet and caring. It made me an emotional wreck. I trembled and faltered for anything to say. In ten years, no one had been interested in finding Crimson, and after so long I had lost hope that anyone, even myself, ever would. When he pulled back to watch me, I closed my eyes to shield against the love that flowed freely through his endless blue ones. It was too intense. I had spent the last decade with a wall against any emotions and Chase was tearing them down every step of the way. It was too much. I didn't want something to lose. Someone to lose. My memories surfaced again and the cold raced through me. Screams of pain and terror from my past filled my head sharply. I suddenly stilled in his arms and pulled back. I spun away from him and sucked in air suddenly out of breath. My heart raced and my palms started to sweat. My wings retracted in sudden emotional confusion disappearing entirely into my back. Escape. I found my way to the laundry room by following the gentle rhythm of the dryer and yanked my clothes out. The jeans were still damp but my black shirt, gray vest, and undies were crisp and warm. I tugged his pants off and shimmied into my undies there in the laundry room. I tugged my jeans on leaving them undone. I yanked the hoodie over my head and tossed it onto the floor with his pants. I snapped my bra into place and felt the hairs on the back of my neck rise. A clump formed in my throat. I felt his presence before he walked in. His eyes burned my naked back. I froze inhaling deep, shaky breaths. He stepped up behind me and traced the markings. When my wings pulled into me, they became a part of my back like a tattoo or a second skin. I could feel his fingertips tumbling over the feathers as he stroked from my shoulder blades to my tail bone. I inhaled deeply trying to keep my body under control. My brain was frantic with emotions while my body was frantic with need. I sucked in a shaky breath.

He suddenly grabbed my hips and sunk his forehead into my shoulder. He sighed. "Is this how it's going to be Crimson?"

I cringed. His voice was so quiet, so solemn.

"You show up when it's convenient for you, and come the next morning you take off like nothing happened. Like nothing touched you."

"Nothing did happen," I whisper.

Another sigh. "Right." He pressed his lips against my neck and pulled away.

It felt so wrong. I turned and watched him start to walk away. His shoulders sagged a little and his head was bent.

I thought about the last three weeks, how miserable I had been. I had tried my hardest to get him out of my head and nothing had worked. How miserable he must have been, thinking about me and not knowing if I would ever show back up and how long I would stick around. I knew ending it now was for the best.

"Chase." I wanted to bite my tongue, but my heart raced instead. He froze when I called his name. He took a deep breath and slowly turned back to me with his eyes closed. When they slitted open and the blues and greens of swirling emotion escaped, he stole my breath. He was just as much of a mess as I was. I put on a shaky smile, standing there in my bra and unzipped blue jeans. "Wanna go for a ride?"

He watched me for a moment, waiting to see if I was kidding, then his lip twitched. "I'll get dressed."

I bit my lip and nodded. He didn't move. My neck heated as he watched my eyes. I held my ground, watching him watch me. It was him that moved first, toward me. My heart raced. He slowly stalked toward me like a hunter approaching his prey. He never paused, just grabbed my head and pulled my lips to his. Then stopped. Just before our lips met, he stopped. I opened my eyes and found his wide open watching me. My skin flushed. I blinked in confusion. "Kiss me, Crimson." His breath heated my lips. I stared into the swirls of green and blue and felt myself falling. I felt him smile. I kissed him. Hard. I surprised him, that much I could tell. I fused my lips to his and dug my fingers into his hair pulling him closer. His body slammed into mine and he wrapped his arms around me. I lost control. I wanted nothing more than to be as close to him as possible. He must have felt the same way because as soon as our tongues met and tangled he pushed me back into the dryer. His hips ground against me and my body burned. His hands found my backside and roughly squeezed pulling a moan from my throat. He lifted me up onto the dryer and stepped into my legs. My heart raced and everything but this man started to fade into the distance. His hands traveling up my back bumping into my bra clasp was what finally snapped me back

71

into reality. I tugged his mouth away gently by his hair. When he opened his eyes they smoldered and cracked like electricity.

I released his hair and shoved him back gently. "You, are very bad for me."

He smiled. "You can add it to your list."

I hopped down and grabbed my shirt tugging it over my head. I tucked it into my jeans and zipped them up. "Smartass." I shoved him again. "Go get ready."

When I walked back into the living room fully clothed, he came out in blue jeans and a black T-shirt. His hair was wet and he smelled like the soap from the shower. I grinned and tossed my vest over the chair.

"Ready?"

"Hell, yeah."

I walked toward the balcony and he followed. When I stepped into the sunshine I grinned. My low-back shirt allowed the warm golden rays to touch my wings. They started to rustle and stretch. I turned back to him as they popped out and spread to their full expanse. He froze to the spot he was standing in and watched in fascination. I smiled and crooked my finger at him. "Over here, Rockstar."

His brow lifted at the second use of his new nickname. I shrugged. He reminded me of a hot rockstar.

Dangerous, wild and full of life. He walked to me and I held out my arms. He stepped into them without hesitation and I wrapped my arms around him. I hugged him tight and whispered against his ear. "Hang on tight."

He wrapped his arms around my waist and tucked his head into my neck.

"I intend to."

I ignored the shiver at his words and waited for him to take a deep breath before bolting straight up into the air with Chase against me.

Chapter 5

I tried to keep the flight smooth and quick. I had no idea how humans did with the flying thing. This time I noticed the small things that he would have noticed. For the first time since I had gotten my wings, I heard the sound of heavy wind pushing against my wings. I noticed the slight whistle as wind blew past my ears. I actually saw the blurs of life far below. His head didn't move from my neck and I feared for a moment that he might be getting sick. I flipped over on my back and he lifted his head. His eyes glowed with wonder and amazement. He smiled brightly and I couldn't help but smile back. I loosened my arms from around his waist and stretched them out to the side. He gripped my waist tightly and I yelled at him to let go. He hesitated then slowly put his arms out beside mine. His fingers locked with mine and squeezed. I smiled and flung my head back gliding across the sky with him above me. The wind caressed me gently and the warm light soothed me, but Chase, he made me feel like I was right where I was meant to be. And it worried me.

My place was only a few miles away from his so we were almost there already. I flipped back over and twisted his arms so that he faced away from me. His hands tightened afraid I might drop him. I wrapped my legs around his waist and my arms over his chest. He watched ahead suddenly interested in where we were going. When I saw my place down below I slowly dropped like a deflating balloon. I checked over the area, to be sure nothing had changed since I left. No new footprints or tire tracks. No broken branches or trampled weeds. No lights in the darkness. I lowered him onto my balcony slowly letting him get his footing. When he was steady I let go. He turned to me with a huge smile on his face and I had to laugh. I pushed open the glass door and stepped into my house. He followed. When the door was shut behind him I let loose the blinds and flipped on the soft lights. They lit up half my bedroom in a soft glowing gold. He looked around. I followed his gaze seeing it as a stranger for the first time. I had no furniture save for a bed and nightstand. I had a small closet but no color and no photos. No, life. I looked at him curious.

"At least the bed makes it look like you actually live here."

I grinned. My bed was a King size cloud. I had at least five plush blankets in black and white scattered across it and three fluffy pillows tossed around.

He stepped around me and out into the hallway inspecting everything as he went. He checked out my bathroom, complete with a room size shower as well as a large tub. "Hmmmmm, guess you get to stretch out a bit more here."

"Yes."

He walked down the hall and investigated the rest of my house, although there wasn't much to see. A lot of bare walls and empty rooms. I sat at the bar and watched him inspect everything. He liked my fireplace in the living room and my extremely clean kitchen. Maybe too clean. He scoffed at my totally empty refrigerator, and cringed at my bare cabinets. "How does someone that likes food as much as you not have any food in your house?"

"I ate it all."

"Just wow."

"Plus I'm never here."

"You still eat."

"Yes, but I prefer what other people make me."

"Why?"

"I'm a terrible cook."

"Guess you're lucky you met me."

"Yet to be determined."

"Burn." He rubbed his chest.

He scanned the area once more and his eyes landed on the one photo that I have in my entire house. It sits on the fireplace mantle. He crooks an eye at me and when I say nothing he slowly walks to it. He stands and studies it.

It is an old photo, about the size of a piece of paper, with the edges crinkled under the glass. One large man with dark hair and glasses stood with a beautiful violet-eyed woman in his arms. They both smiled happily at the four children seated beside them. Three boys -- in various ages from about five to sixteen. All brown haired and chocolate eyed with happy grins. One teenage girl about eighteen, dark hair and violet eyes with a smile that radiated love and happiness.

He looks back at me and I know that he recognizes the girl. He opens his mouth, but I shake my head and he stops. I'm not going to walk down that road. He quickly scans the room taking in the emptiness. "Homey."

I smile. "Smartass."

"So how come you don't keep your bike in your living room?"

I nod my head towards a door and start that way with him following me. We walk down a small flight of stairs and when I flip the switch at the landing his eyes widen. Where my house is bare and empty my basement is brimming with life. I keep music playing all the time so when we enter the area Rihanna is singing about being friends with the monsters under her bed. The walls are lined with tool boxes that are brimming with tools. I have wrenches, screwdrivers, socket sets, compressors, air drills, and even paint guns.

In the center sits my custom made Wind Runner. She is electric blue with chrome stretching across every metal surface. Dark black tires and snake eye blue headlights. I had the name 'Titanium' in diamond plated chrome attached to each side of the gas tank, as well as a wing curving around each side of the seat. The bike had been my first purchase after my wake-up call about five years ago. My first get-my-shit-together purchase. The second had been the house, so I had somewhere to put the bike.

Chase whistles behind me.

I turn to look at him. "Surprised?"

"Nothing from you surprises me." He walked around the room a bit. "I just need to get used to your many sides." He kept walking. "Was this a self-taught hobby?"

"My dad," a lump started in my throat. "I was a daddy's girl."

He looked at me interested in the sudden and new information. I looked away and went to the bike. I turned the key and pushed the button. It purred to life. He came toward me.

"How did you learn to ride?" I asked him needing a subject change.

"My uncle. He is real big into bikes and taught me everything I know."

I looked at him with surprise. "So where's yours?"

"Got T-boned last year, broken leg, broken arm, and fractured skull. New one isn't in the budget yet."

I looked at him surprised. For some reason the idea of him getting hurt nudged me a little. I grabbed two pairs of sunglasses from a small compartment on the side. "Guess you need to sell some more pics." I handed him one set.

"Guess we need to take some more then." He grinned putting them on. "I made a killing off the Biker Angel photos."

I put my own sunglasses on and thought about what I had told the man in the liquor store. "Perhaps."

I hopped on the seat and sat up for him to sit behind me. He settled in and I sat back. For some reason, it spiked my body temp up quite a bit. Could have been from us sitting together so closely. Could have been because he wrapped both arms around my waist and dug his nose into my hair inhaling deeply. Could have been because of the beast that was currently purring between my legs. I shook my thoughts trying to get my brain back on track. I pushed the small button by the brake and the garage door smoothly lifted up.

I hit the radio and Katy Perry's Dark Horse blasted from the speakers. I smiled. It was fitting. We grumbled out of the garage and I pushed the button again.

Katy's voice echoed around us asking the boy if they wanted to play with magic. A clear warning in the silence around us.

I paused at the end of the drive. I turned my head to the side until his nose touched my cheek. "Ready, Rockstar?"

"Born ready, Angel."

I smiled and hit the throttle making the tires scream out the drive. I let her run wide open down the quiet street. There weren't any other houses on this road. I owned several acres, refusing to sell to developers. So I had a nice quiet street within five miles of the busy city.

I sang along to the music, belting out about the perfect storm and not being able to go back. I felt his arms tighten around me and I smiled. I cranked the gas again so that we were flying faster and faster away from the city. He didn't ask where we were going, didn't comment on my speed, just held on tight slowly breathing against my ear. I had no destination in mind, just needed to escape reality and I let the wheels carry us farther and farther away into the sunlight.

We came to a burger joint about two hours away just as the sun was starting to descend towards the western horizon. I pointed at it and I felt him nod against my shoulder. I slowed down my speed and cut into the lot. It was a hole in the wall, but having eaten here before I knew the food was decent. I parked my bike right outside the window and hit the kill switch. I sat forward to let him up, but his hands dug deep into my hips. He pulled me back against him so I turned my head to see what he needed. His hand reached up and grabbed my chin to hold me still while his lips covered mine. It was a short kiss, but it was just as hot as before. Tangled everything in my head up again. When he pulled back and smiled I frowned at him. "Bad."

"Very bad, but you love it."

I huffed and swung my leg over the handlebars. I didn't wait for him, just stomped to the door with irritation. I heard him chuckle behind me and it irritated me even more. I found an empty table by the window, parked my butt and picked up a menu. There were maybe ten people sitting around the little place which was how I liked it. Not too many people to make me feel overwhelmed. Chase saw me and headed toward the back where a restroom sign hung. The waitress came before he came back so I ordered two root beers without ice remembering his choice of drink at the diner when I first met him. He came back just as she was bringing them to the table. He raised a brow at the frothing glass. "Good guess."

"Good memory," I replied matter of factually.

He tried to recall how I knew that, but came up blank. "So what does the woman that faces all evil with a smile, sings while riding her motorcycle, and kisses like the world ends tomorrow eat for dinner?"

My neck flushes. Is that really how I kiss?"I guess it depends on if it is a good smile, good singing, and good kissing?"

He grins. "Smile is a killer. Singing, Iv'e heard worse. Kissing, you will never in a million years hear a complaint from me."

"I didn't think so."

"So, food?"

"Burgers are good, fries are hot and ice cream is yummy."

He set his menu down. "Sounds good to me."

The waitress returned and smiled over-the-top happily at Chase. She reintroduced herself for his especial convenience and gushed excitedly while blushing. I rolled my eyes. Do people actually act like this on purpose? It was irritating and lame.

I ignored her and ordered a burger with cheese only, fries with a side of brown gravy and vanilla ice cream. She wrote it down with a sour face and returned to Chase with a smile. I cocked up an eyebrow at him interested if he was noticing the little show. He watched me instead of watching her.

"The same."

When she left I rolled my eyes again.

"Plain cheeseburger?" He asked. "No lettuce, no onion, no tomato, no nothing?"

I looked at him. "What do I look like? A damn rabbit?"

"Interesting. I guess I pictured the badass, evil slaying, biker angel to go for the steak and mashed potatoes with an extra side of mashed potatoes."

"I had that yesterday."

He paused, then grinned. "Of course you did."

"So if you sing while riding your bike, do you also sing while working on it?"

"Yup."

"In the shower?"

"Yup."

"How come you don't sing in my shower?"

"First time I was drunk, second time I would have split my own head open."

"Will there be a next time? In the near future?"

My lips twitched. Sneaky. "Possibility."

"Good to know. So what do you do in between pissing off bad guys and riding your bike?"

"Eat."

"Sounds great," he said dryly.

"It is."

"How do you afford it?"

"Haven't you heard? I recently took up a modeling career."

The waitress chose that moment to set our food on the table. She glared at me and smiled at Chase.

"Interesting," he ignored her and continued to watch me. "Who is your manager?"

"I dunno," I shrugged. "Some guy I met at a bar."

"Technically I think we met at a diner." He popped a few fries in his mouth.

"Technically," I waited until she came back with our gravy. "I think we officially met back at your apartment, the morning after when you were playing Doctor." She slopped a bit of his gravy on the table and I smiled.

"Oh yeah, that was the day you did that modeling for me."

The girl stuck her nose in the air and walked away. I watched her go with satisfaction. He just shook his head and returned to his food. I had eaten almost everything before he started talking again. "Do you do this a lot?"

"Come here? Only a few times."

"No. Just take off on your bike for a few hours?"

"Yeah, I guess." I thought about it. Several times a month, and in the last few weeks, almost every day. "Why?"

"Just curious."

When my plate was empty the girl returned with our ice cream and all but threw it onto the table. "Pleasant."

He shrugged.

I took a huge glob of ice cream and dropped it into my root beer. He raised a brow and his lips lifted. "That explains the absence of ice."

It was my turn to shrug and I watched as he dropped his own glob into his soda.

It was after I finished my float that I recognized the guy sitting at the bar watching me. When our eyes met he smiled. "Shit," I whispered.

Chase raised his eyebrows in question but didn't have to wait long.

The man came strolling over. "Titan!" He plundered down next to me in the booth and smiled like a kid with a lollipop.

"Marco," I replied drily.

"Damn girl, how long has it been?"

"Not long enough."

Chase watched us without comment. I could see the curiosity in his eyes.

"Come on now, you know you missed your best buddy."

"Yup, just like a zit."

He laughed and his eyes settled on Chase. "She's hilarious."

He smiled and shrugged.

"Now who is this guy you're hanging out with?" He eyed Chase up.

"Chase, Marco. Marco, Chase."

They both nodded at each other. Marco then turned his conversation to Chase. "So how do you know my girl here?"

He smiled at the clear attempt of ownership. "We just keep running into each other."

"Really? So tell me, how close are you two?"

I broke in before Chase could answer. "I've taken up modeling. He's my manager." I ignored the flash in his eyes.

Marco watched the exchange without comment.

"Wait." He thought for a moment. His eyes widened and he pointed at me.

"Biker Angel?"

I rolled my eyes. "You couldn't come up with a better name?"

Chase shrugged, "I'll work on it."

Marco grinned. "I can't believe I didn't recognize you! I like the one that looks like you're about to crea.."

"Marco," I warned.

"Sorry. So what are you, Chase?"

Chase looked at him confused. "Sorry?"

"Well I'm not seeing any fangs, and you're not striking me as demonic so that leaves angel or warlock."

"I'm not any..."

I cut him off, "we were just leaving."

Again his eyes flashed but he didn't comment.

Marco just smiled. "Well alright, but don't be a stranger Red, you know you can call me for anything."

"Uh huh." I motioned to the waitress. She rolled her eyes at me. She brought the check without comment and I threw a bunch of bills on the table before standing.

Marco turned his attention to Chase. "Chase." He nodded.

Chase nodded in return. "Marco."

Marco smiled at us then headed for the bathroom pulling his cell out of his pocket as he went. I hurried out the door with Chase on my heels. When we were outside I swore again. "What's the problem?" He asked me while he sat on the bike. I didn't respond, just jumped on in front of him and cranked the motor. We threw stones leaving the lot and I sped as fast as possible down the road back towards the city. I was tense and I knew he could feel it. After about ten minutes of dangerous driving, even for me, he yelled against my ear. "You wanna clue me in here before you kill both of us!" I swore and looked around us. Seeing nothing I pulled to the side of the road and stopped with a jerk. I left the bike run and sat thinking for a minute. He put his hand on my shoulder and I all but hissed at him. "Shit, Crimson. What's got you all worked up?"

I took a deep breath. I spun my head back at him. "Marco is a snitch for hire. He gets info on anyone and everyone and sells it to the right person."

"What? You really think anyone cares that you started modeling?"

"He wasn't interested in me, he was interested in you."

He paused. "What do you mean?"

"Think about it, Rockstar. I am the wanted woman, the Titanium Angel. Everyone wants me for themselves. I never had anything they could use against me."

It took a moment, but it clicked. "Until now…"

I nodded once. "He probably just called about ten big wigs to inform them of my new human plaything." I cranked my head to look him in the eye. "Now, if they can't get me, they will come after you."

He was silent so I turned back and cranked the throttle until we were speeding back toward the city once again. He didn't comment any more on my dangerous driving.

We almost made it home. We were about twenty minutes from my place when I saw them standing in the road ahead. I swore and slowed. "Chase."

He brought his face up close to mine. "If anything happens, you take this bike and you get the fuck out of here."

"What? Hell no I'm not leaving you..."

I hissed. "Listen! I'm a hell of a lot sturdier than you. You're human. You can get killed! If things get ugly you get the hell out. Just do not go home. Do not go to my house or any of your friends places. They will probably follow you."

He swore. "What about you?"

"I'm a big girl."

He swore again. I stopped about fifty yards away and let the bike idle. I left the lights on and hopped off, slowly walking toward them. There were three of them. Looked like one was demon since I could see his eyes glowing red in the short distance and the other two were probably vamps judging by their huge size. My wings which had been contently quiet all afternoon started to twitch beneath my skin. Danger. I walked in

90

the light slowly checking out my opponents. The demon looked like he would be my biggest problem. Definitely a class three demon, one of the crazy inside and out guys. Although the vamps were stronger, they were stupider. The demon lacked strength but held pure evil in his grasp. This was going to get rough. I stopped halfway and waited. It wasn't long before all three started charging me. I stooped down and gained my steady footing. I raised my arms and barred my teeth. When they were halfway to me I snatched a crystal dagger from the air beside me as well as a pistol. Cool, I know. An angel thing. I think. I fired twice at the demon's head to slow him down and raised my blade against the vamp that reached me first. He avoided my swing and knocked me against the leg. I kicked him in the knee and shot at the second vamp when he came at me. The demon was still waiting for his head to grow back. The first vamp stood back up with a wobble in his leg and punched me in the thigh. I swore, pretty sure I had a fractured bone now. I punched him with my dagger hand in the mouth and my hand burned with pain. He smiled at me with a dark purple blood flowing from his lips. I smiled back and shot him in the head close range, then I sliced his head off. The other vamp charged me, knocking me to the ground and the oxygen from my lungs. I sucked in a gulp of air and kicked him off of me.

The demon's head was starting to grow back because I heard him screaming in rage. The vamp swung at me again and I stuck my dagger in his arm. He yelled and swung with the other arm. He nailed me in the jaw and I saw stars. My wings fluttered angrily against me and I let them loose. The vamp watched as they stretched out and expanded to their full span. With a little twitch of my wrist the feathers turned into razor blades. His eyes widened and I didn't give him a chance to beg, my wings attacked him cutting off his screams as they circled him. When he was staked and out of my way I searched for the demon. It was quiet. I looked back toward Chase who still sat on the bike watching me. When my eyes found his the demon jumped me from above. He tore into my wing with his claws. I screamed in pain and outrage. My wing burned like fire and it slashed back and forth. I jammed my dagger back into his gut and spun around when he fell back. He cried out and lunged at me. I shot him again in the chest. It didn't have any effect. I bit my lip in pain and tasted my own blood. The demon watched me while we circled each other. "Why don't you invite your human to come play Lost One?" His voice was eerie and dark. It crept across me like the legs of thousands of bugs crawling across my skin.

"Why don't you focus so I can kick your ass?"

He hissed. "Come on now, I could have some fun with him."

I cringed. Not on my watch. My good wing stabbed toward it and sliced into its chest. Bright red steaming liquid poured out. I shot it in the head again and stabbed it in the chest with my dagger. It screamed in fury and I pulled my blade out.

I started to run towards the bike when the demon fell on its face. It would at least buy us some time.

When Chase saw me coming, he kicked the bike into gear and spun toward me. I jumped on behind him while he sped away and I watched the lifeless forms until they were a speck in the distance. I tucked away all my weapons into the air that I had retrieved them from and cringed when my wing burned again. I tried to tuck it away into my skin, but I hissed when it burned more.

Chase drove as fast as he could, I had no intention of stopping him. He slowed by my road but I shook my head and told him to go to his place. He needed to go home and get away from me. When we pulled onto his street I told him to park a few blocks down. He slowed into a spot and killed the engine. He jumped off and spun around grabbing my face. He slowly inspected my split lip and ran his eyes over the rest of me. He gingerly touched my torn wing and it trembled. It would heal but it would take a day or two. I watched the street for any sign of movement. The only thing I had spotted so far was a wild cat in the alley. When he was done playing Doctor I whispered. "Go home Chase." He paused. "I'll watch 'til you get up there. If everything is good come to the balcony."

He didn't move and his eyes locked on my face. "You're angry with yourself aren't you?"

"Yes."

"Because you think you've put me in danger."

"I have put you in danger."

He swore. "In this world everything is dangerous. Frankly for you I'm willing to face the danger."

"This is not a joke."

"No, it's not. But you're not taking the blame for this. Everything is about taking risks, it's part of living."

I did not answer.

"You don't intend on coming back do you?"

I said nothing.

He swore again. "Well when you decide that maybe it's time to start living again, you know where to find me." He spun around and stomped away angrily.

I watched him go trying to keep myself together. Why did it hurt so much? He was just a human. I watched as he marched down the sidewalk and disappeared inside. I watched the skies, I watched the street and I watched the windows for movement from other apartments. Nothing moved. The light from his balcony switched on and he came outside. He rested his arms against the rail and watched me. We stood like this for awhile. Me, sitting on my bike staring into the tiny specs of blue, and him, watching me from above. It was a stalemate. Him, hoping I would change my mind, and me, knowing that taking this any further would be like signing his death warrant.

I cranked the engine and purred out of the spot and down the street heading back home. I watched on my way home too. To be sure no one followed. I checked my house as I always do for signs of life and found none. I sighed deeply when I was parked back in my basement. After sitting and listening to my music for a moment, I trudged up to my bath and stripped to my skin. I turned on my shower to scalding hot and stepped under the spray. I let my wings unfurl. The one still burned and was only able to stretch about halfway. The other sensed the distress and balanced itself out. I groaned when the water seared the wound in my wing. My wings trembled and my body shivered. When I shut my eyes I saw the demon getting Chase. I pictured the things it would have done to him and I shook. Memories scored my brain and iced over my skin. The screams from my past echoed around me bouncing off the tile walls. The hot water stopped chasing away the cold and I squeezed my eyes shut trying to block the memories out. When it didn't work I cranked the water as hot as it would go feeling the burn on my skin but it still did not penetrate the ice inside me. I sat down on the tile floor tucking my head and arms in to let the hot water beat the cold from my body.

Chapter 6

I woke from a dead sleep when someone called out to me. I blinked in the darkness of my bedroom and rubbed my eyes. At first my body tensed wondering who was here, then I heard the voice again, in my head. I had a moment of wonder if I had actually heard something. I shook my head to shake out the sleepiness and waited. Sure enough it came again. Chase? It was his voice, but why was it in my head? I crawled away from the soft warmth of my bed and stood up stretching my body. It had only been three days since I had dropped him off at home, and every night he had haunted my dreams. Sometimes, they were good dreams. Hot sex and warm smiles. Others were not good. Danger, blood, and pain. So I was kind of used to hearing him in my sleep, but this sounded so sad. And he called me by my real name. Maybe it was my mind playing tricks on me or maybe he really was crying out to me. Maybe he was in trouble. I was standing there debating what to do when he made a strangled cry of desperation and my heart leaped into my throat. I shoved open the door to my balcony and shot into the air.

I was at his apartment in minutes and dropped to his balcony. The windows were dark and the night was silent. My wings shivered with the eerie quiet. The door was slightly ajar just as it had been the night of his party. I slipped into the darkness and looked around. Nothing. I slowly crept inside and tiptoed down the hall. I heard muffled cries from his bedroom. I waited outside listening for more, my muscles strained ready for anything and when I could wait no more I pushed the door open. My eyes adjusted instantly to the room. The windows were cracked letting in a light breeze and silver moonlight. I found Chase twisted up in black sheets on his bed. His body was taut and his eyes squeezed tightly shut. Sweat beaded his brow and chest. My heart twisted when I realized his dreams were just as troubled as mine. Then my body quivered in yearning. I stepped back away from him and he cried out to me. "Crimson!"

It racked my body hearing it out loud and in my head at once. Like an echo that rips into your soul. My legs moved toward the bed and my hands reached out for him. I hesitated for only a second before my fingers touched his arm. His body froze and I whispered to him. "Chase."

In the darkness his eyes popped open revealing mesmerizing blue oceans. The moonlight glinted off them like they do the waves and he watched me. Neither of us moved. My heart pumped erratically and my breaths were short and uneven. I could feel his blood pumping beneath my fingertips. He blinked and his eyes searched my face while he sucked in long breaths of air. Relief softened his expression and his eyes travelled from my head to my knees. I flushed. I just had to wear a little lacy black number to bed on the night he chose to call out to me. The scant two-piece had been a good idea when I had planned another rough night of loneliness between my own sheets.

My fingers retracted from his arm as my skin tingled with goosebumps. Warning bells suddenly started screaming in my head. This was bad, very, very bad. My brain told my feet to turn and run, but my body wasn't responding. I was glued to the floor, staring into his eyes. His eyes started to focus and he licked his lips. My mouth went dry. My feet finally took a step back and he noticed. His body slowly uncoiled from the bed. The sheets fell from his skin with a whisper. He wore only a pair of dark boxer briefs. The cotton stretched across him. Another step back. His eyes tracked me. He stood to full height towering over me slightly. He assessed the distance from me to the door in a quick scan. I once again felt like the prey being hunted. I straightened my back and tucked my wings in. He followed my movements as I still inched my way back. He took a slow step in my direction and my breath caught. I twirled around and lunged for the door, but when I got there it was already shut. It was shut and I found myself pressed up against it. With a heated mass of man behind me. My arms were pulled behind me as my wings contracted into my skin and my legs were forced apart with his knee. My breathing was choppy and my skin on fire. Anywhere his body pressed against mine I was melting into liquid gold.

His nose dug into my hair and he inhaled deeply. I whimpered. Crap. I felt him smile against my shoulder and he grabbed my hair with one hand and gently tugged my head back. He softly kissed my cheek and I closed my eyes. His lips traveled down onto my neck and his tongue lashed out to taste me right above the pounding flesh of my neck. I trembled.

"Chase," I whispered.

He ignored me and his lips traveled along my shoulder and down my arm. He kissed me where my wings started and they quivered. He stroked them with his nose and I felt myself starting to purr like a cat. His lips kissed them and my knees started to shake. He tugged me around pushed my back against the door.

He kissed me gently on the lips while holding my hands prisoner with one of his. His other hand still held my hair keeping my head where he wanted it. "Crimson," he whispered against my lips.

"Chase, this is a bad idea." I dug deep in my head for some sanity.

"It's a terrible idea." His lips traveled along my neck to my collar bone.

"When have you ever not done something because it was a bad idea?"

Got me. "Since I met you."

His lips curved into another smile against the top of the valley between my breasts. My breath stilled. His tongue streaked out and slid horizontal along the black lace just above my nipple. I whimpered again. "Crimson," his lips whispered along my skin. "Stay with me."

I slowly shook my head trying to pull out my last bit of sense. His head came back up and his eyes found mine. I lost myself in blue swirls and green streaks. His thigh pushed between my legs and rubbed. I sucked in a gasp of air and his lips covered mine again for a searing heart throbbing kiss. His leg pushed into me and came back. And again. My body started melting from the inside out. Every part of me rose in a blinding heat and I couldn't find my way down. I didn't want to. My hands were still held captive behind my back, I could have easily broken free, but I let him hold me there. When my body started to lose resistance he froze. His eyes found mine again. "Crimson." I watched the moonlight glint against his eyes. "Kiss me."

I squeezed my eyes shut and took a deep breath. He didn't move. I was standing on an edge and had to either fly or fall. He released my hands slowly, hesitant but giving me the choice. I slit open my eyes and smiled at him. I whispered, "Are you sure you want to play with magic?" His eyes lit fire and his smile turned dangerous. My wings unfurled with impatience and surrounded him. They pulled him to me and only when my arms were wrapped around him did I finally let go. I kissed him like I was starving for him and needed only him to survive. His fingers dug into my hips and mine tangled in his hair. Our tongues lashed against each other and my lips burned with the pressure. His hands rounded my bottom and lifted me against him. I hopped up and wrapped my legs around his waist letting our centers press together. He moaned against my lips. My wings pushed against the door behind me and he turned and walked to the bed dropping down with me. When we landed his center pushed harder against me and it was my turn to moan. It had been so long and my body was racing for him. I wanted him and I wanted him now. "Chase." I pleaded against his lips. He ground his hips harder into me. I moaned again. His lips raced down my throat and his mouth covered my lace covered nipple. My body zinged with electricity and I bowed off the bed. His hands found the zipper between my breasts and tugged it down to my belly button. His eyes feasted while the lace slowly spread open for him to see. With that gone all that covered me was the tiny black shorts that were not even proper bathing suit bottoms. He pulled them down and swiftly tossed them away. Then he just watched me. My cheeks flushed. I knew I had a decent figure. Lots of guys had told me so back in my rebel days, but for some reason only right now with this man mattered. Even though he had already seen most of this, I still held my breath waiting for his reaction.

"Crimson." He whispered looking into my eyes. "You are phenomenal."

Relief washed over me and before I could come up with a smartass remark his mouth covered my breast. My body bowed up towards him again and his hands went to work exploring my body. They trailed flames over my skin leaving me burning everywhere he touched. Then his tongue would follow and wet the flames. The gentle breeze from the window became my only relief from the fire. I was starting to lose control of my body and my arms fell to the bed sheets. When his hands started to explore my center, I dug my nails into the sheets holding on tight for any kind of level ground.

He built me up so high that my eyes started to lose focus. I couldn't concentrate. I pleaded again, "Chase, please."

He moved away for a second then his lips found mine again. "Say it again." He moved between my legs and my body trembled in excitement.

I swallowed, my mouth suddenly dry. "Chase, please."

"Again," he demanded.

"Ch..." he pushed into me and I screamed in pleasure. "...ase!!!!" I gasped as he shoved in as far as our bodies would allow and still I wanted more. I wrapped my legs around him and pulled him farther in. He moaned loudly. He froze taking it all in and I still wanted more. I used my strength and flipped us both so that I straddled him. His hands dug into my thighs and my wings fluttered. They stretched out above us as I started to move against him. Within moments I had built us both into a frenzy and was reaching the edge. I kissed him hard and let his hands dig into my hips. When I lifted he pulled, slamming me back down and going that much farther. I straightened my back and pushed my chest out tilting my head back and just feeling every movement. I felt his body coil beneath me and I tightened my center slamming back down with a scream of ecstasy. I heard him call out as he fell off the edge of sanity right behind me.

Chapter 7

I blinked at the sunlight that blazed brightly through the window. Morning already? I moaned when I tried to move. Everything burned. I smiled. It was a fantastic burn, a completely worth it burn. I moved my head around to study my surroundings. I was butt naked sleeping diagonally across Chase's bed with only a sliver of a sheet twisted around my hips covering all the important stuff. My chest, on the other hand, was perked right up for anyone to see. I would have moved to cover it, but my body screamed at the thought of moving. My wings had tucked themselves away at some point through the night. Not that I recalled when. I actually could not recall much of anything except having the most mind-blowing sex of my life, several times. Each time through the night, it had been Chase waking me up with a few tongue flicks in sensitive spots or finger strokes in the right places and that had been all it took to have me ready and willing. I smiled.

A whistle blew softly across the room. I turned my head and found him leaning against the doorway with his hands tucked into blue jean pockets and his wet hair dripping down his naked chest. My body responded. Down Girl. I leaned up on one elbow and rested my chin in my hand.

"If I could walk into my bedroom and have that view every morning I would die a happy man."

"Really?"

"Definitely."

"Even in twenty years."

"Even in fifty years."

"Hmmmm, let's just deal with the day for now."

"For now."

I rolled my eyes at him. He stays there watching me so I groan and crawl out of the bed. Muscles screamed and limbs ached. I walk naked toward him as his eyes travel along my skin. When he doesn't move, I smile.

"Food?"

"Is that all you think about?"

"Pretty much."I agreed. "That and this." I grabbed his head and pulled him to me for a hot desperate kiss.

When I let him go, he is disoriented. "I can deal with that."

I chuckle and head for the shower.

I started humming a random song that was stuck in my head as the hot water soothed all my muscles. The back of my neck tingled just before I heard his soft footsteps come into the bathroom. "Your choices for this morning are scrambled eggs or grilled cheese. I have been severely negligent on my grocery shopping tasks."

I peeked my head out and smiled. "Both?"

"Alright, but then I have to go get some food."

"I'll go with you."

"Are you volunteering so that you can spend time with me or so that you can pick out more food?"

"Both?" I grinned again.

He rolled his eyes but left the room with a smile.

After my shower, I put my black set back on considering I had only worn them for an hour at most and found the clothing that I wore last time sitting on his dresser. I shimmied the skinny jeans on and pulled the hoodie over my head. I looked under the sink and found a brand new big toothed comb sitting next to the tiny black one. I paused for a minute. Had he got this just for me? I took a deep breath and wondered just what I was actually getting myself into. I grabbed the comb and followed the smell of melted cheese down the hall. I sat on the edge of the couch to rip out all of the knots while Chase continued cooking. It was quiet, but neither of us seemed to mind. I started humming the tune that was still stuck in my head and finished smoothing out my mess. The bigger comb made the task much easier and I leaned back on the couch still humming and staring out into space.

"Is that what I think it is?"

I focused my attention and turned toward him. "Hmmmm?"

He walked toward me and leaned over me on the couch. "You do know that it is only October right?"

I watched him with confusion. "Yeah?"

He leaned down until his lips were only a breath from mine. His eyes glowed with laughter. "It's not beginning to look a lot like Christmas."

Crap. Was that what I was singing? I crinkled my brow at him. "Actually, it's almost November."

He laughed and his lips touched mine in a brief 'you're cute' kiss.

He grabbed my hands and pulled me up. "Let's eat."

I followed. You don't have to tell me twice when food is involved.

We sat eating in a comfortable silence when I noticed him grinning at me.

"What?"

"I can't wait to see you after Thanksgiving. You are probably one of those people that put up your tree two months early and sings Christmas music constantly."

I tried to scowl at him, but I failed miserably. "I like Christmas music. I can't help it that I plant it into my head all year round." He smiled and I looked away. "As for the tree, I don't do that anymore."

He choked. He looked up in amazement. "You don't put up a tree?"

"Nope."

"Why not?"

I shrugged. "Just don't, haven't in about ten years."

I stuffed my mouth and let him get it. It clicked. I saw the light come on in his brain. He didn't say anymore.

We ate in an awkward silence now. It only took a moment for him to try and fill the silence. "Random question, what exactly is Marco?"

My brow rose with his sudden curiosity. "Dark Angel."

His brow arched with surprise. "And he ratted you out?"

"Hell, yes, he did. Money talks."

"But you're part Dark Angel, why would he throw you under the bus?"

I raised a brow. "I never said I was part Dark Angel."

He shrugged. "Part Dark, part Light. I guessed."

I let it go. "Race has nothing to do with allegiance." I finished my food and sat back. "You could be my brother and you could still feel no allegiance to me. With the way things are right now, a demon could be your best friend and an Angel of Light your enemy."

"That's confusing. I always thought that races stuck together."

"That's the fairytale they teach you in school. That people get along and the Good trump Evil. That the light is always good and the dark is always bad. In this world, nothing is definite and nothing is the way it should be. I'm proof of that."

He looked at me with confusion. "So who is in charge?"

"In a perfect happy world? God. In a fair world? God and Satan in perfect balance. In our world? It's a constant battle, the scale always tipping one way or the other."

"Doesn't sound very stable."

I shrugged. "It is the way it is. Think of the globe going straight up and down. North is God, South is Satan. The angels reign just beneath each of them followed by a mixture of demons, vamps, and warlocks. Humans are the equator, constantly falling in each direction. But each end holds the same amount of power, a game of balance. There is nothing holding anyone together, no single person that each race follows without fail. Nothing and no one to bind them. No middle man to keep the peace. So they do the only thing they can, each side races to build its numbers. They direct humans in certain directions and they make allegiances, through any means possible. Money, sex, force, whatever it takes."

"So a demon can be good?"

I smile at him. "Rare, but possible. Demons, vamps, witches and warlocks all can live among humans peacefully. They blend in. Some become teachers, writers, or librarians." I raised a brow. "Photographers, construction workers and chefs. Whatever they choose, so long as they fit in. It's when they start running around with knives and guns that they start to cause problems. When appetites suddenly involve innocent people and mass murdering occurs. Then, the balance is disturbed and Good retaliates. Which is almost all the time. You could say that my need to demolish scum is my Light Angel side pushing me to do its job." I pushed my chair back. "Everything and everyone eventually falls to one side of the scale, and no one knows until they get there."

"So," he whispered. "Where does a Forgotten fit in?"

"We don't." I stood and walked around a little. "I don't belong on either side of the scale, and it scares the shit outta them."

"Who?"

"Everyone."

"So you being different scares them?"

"Change scares people. It isn't normal to be on both sides. You can't stand with one foot on land and the other on water, your foot falls through the water until it also stands on the ground. A bird cannot live beneath the waves and a fish cannot live in the clouds. One cannot pledge their hearts to good and evil, without somehow breaking a vow to the other. When the moon rises, the sun falls and vice versa. It is one way or the other, there is no normalcy in choosing both."

"So they want the Titanium Angel under their palm because you are both. Because they are scared of you, and because they think they can pull you in one direction."

I nodded. "I am the only living Dark and Light Angel. I am extremely powerful and perhaps with the right persuasion..." I shrugged. "Who knows."

"Ok, Light Angels want you working with them. Dark Angels want you working for them. Vampires...?"

"Special girl, special blood."

"Gotcha, witches and warlocks?"

"Healing abilities, magical blood," I cringe, "body parts."

"Demons?"

"You never know. A demon is the most unpredictable of races, besides me of course. I just avoid the quiet ones and hack the annoying ones."

He sat back in his chair watching me. Silence stretched. "So why don't you go into hiding and blend in like the others?"

I sighed. "Can't. As soon as I set down roots, someone would find me. That's why my house is so empty. I might have to pick up and run at any time. The chase is never ending. So long as the Lost One lives, they search for me."

He sat quietly for another minute before clearing his head and trying to change the subject.

"So what do you usually do on a day like today?"

I considered. "Go for a ride." He smiled and shook his head. He stood up and grabbed the plates.

"What do you do for a living?"

I paused. "Kill things."

"No, how do you make money?"

"I don't need to."

He looked at me incredulously. "Don't angels even need money to survive around here?" He smiled. "Especially one with an appetite like yours?"

I sighed. This divulging of personal information was hard compared to the history lesson. "My parents were loaded. Now, I'm loaded." As an afterthought, I added, "and I don't eat that much."

He looked at me with a slight grin, and didn't comment. Good, he was learning where to tread carefully. "My parents are both doctors, but they are overseas working with the government. I don't see or hear from them much. Just a postcard or phone call every couple months."

I remembered that he was close to his uncle. "What about your uncle?"

He smiled. "He is crazy. My Mom's brother. He was basically who raised me when my parents were busy or out of town, which was basically always. He is great, lives about ten minutes away. Was more concerned about me than my bike last year, which surprised me. I had expected him to be livid, but he wasn't. Said he was just glad I was alright. My parents, on the other hand, were more upset about the bike because they had given me a good chunk of the money to buy it."

I raised my brow. Interesting.

He shrugged and dried his hands with the towel. "Ready to go shopping, Angel?"

I raised a brow again. Was I ever going to escape these nicknames? My belly might have fluttered a little when it came from him, but I ignored it.

He grabbed a jacket and handed me my vest that was hanging by the door. I didn't even remember leaving it here. I pulled it on and he paused. "One question." I froze at his serious tone. "What exactly were you wearing when you rushed over here last night?"

I smiled. "What do you think?"

His eyes widened and I pulled open the door and walked out grinning.

We walked down the hall and into the elevator. He was still silent.

"Surprised?"

"Not surprised, just pissed that I missed it!"

I laughed out loud. "Actually, I am pretty sure you did not miss anything."

His eyes went from light to dark and burning in an instant. My stomach fluttered again. The elevator rang, and I practically ran out the door and through the lobby. He started walking down the sidewalk and I followed.

He headed for a parking lot on the side of the building and pulled out a set of keys. I heard the click of unlocking doors and spotted a black sleek little car with its parking lights flashing. It wasn't pretty, but it wasn't butt ugly. I suppose it could have been worse. He opened the passenger door for me, and I would have blushed if the wind had not chosen that moment to bitterly blow across my face. I ducked inside quickly. He shut the door and walked around. When he was settled in beside me, he noticed my shivers. "Cold?"

I nodded.

"Strange."

"Why?"

"Just never thought my badass angel could get cold."

"Angels don't." I looked at him. "I'm not an angel." He started the engine. "I hate the cold."

"Do you?"

"Absolutely."

"Interesting."

We drove down the street and I watched out the window. I couldn't even tell you the last time I sat in a vehicle. The silence stretched until we pulled into the supermarket lot. He parked and my stomach grumbled.

His brow raised, "I'm going to regret this, aren't I?"

I grinned evilly. "Absolutely."

He sighed and I pushed open my door. I walked quickly inside trying to escape the cold. I waited inside for him while he retrieved a cart from outside the door where they were lined up and chained together. I skipped through all the chips and candy until we hit the snacks. He grabbed one or two things on the way past while following me. I went for some cereal and breakfast bars. He watched everything I chose as if it fascinated him so I grabbed a few normal things like peanut butter and fruit snacks. I rounded the corner and was checking out the baking goods while he got stuck choosing his own cereal. I was debating between a cinnamon muffin mix and a honey cornbread mix when I heard someone call out his name.

"Chase, how's it going?" A deep male voice carried across the aisle.

"Jay," Chase replied without enthusiasm.

"Dude, what the hell are you up to?"

"Oh, not much, just grabbing some food."

"What are you doing with your life nowadays?"

"Oh, not too much, Jay." Still I sensed no interest in this person or conversation.

"Too bad. I just got into a nice law firm. Nice boss, nicer daughter." He said this with a chuckle. "Last I heard you wrecked that new bike last year and you were scraping by with that little camera of yours. That must suck ass. No bike, no job and no girl." The male voice laughed out loud.

I heard a mumbled reply from Chase and decided that I was not fond of this Jay guy and that maybe I should intervene.

I spotted whipped topping in the cooler door and grabbed a can then glided back to the first aisle. I saw the Jay guy standing by Chase smiling like an idiot while Chase just stood by the cart not looking at him. I spotted the chocolate syrup and grabbed a bottle. I did my best sexy smile and walked toward them. "Babe, which do you prefer?" Both heads snapped up and their eyes widened. I held up both bottles. "Edible undies, or chocolate lollipops?" I said this with a slight whisper so only they would hear me.

Luckily Chase was able to get over his surprise rather quickly and go with it. "Both. Definitely both."

"Great!" I dropped both into the cart with a sexy grin and sauntered away.

"Holy shit, was that Biker Angel?" I heard the surprise and jealousy even from the next aisle.

"Yes, yes it was." I heard the grin that was plastered on his face in his voice.

"Wait, you took those pictures?"

"I sure did."

"Wow."

Sounded like Jay was at a loss for words. I smiled. After a moment when it sounding like neither of them were moving I called over, "Chase, how about some pudding?"

"Sounds good," he called back over. "See you around Jay."

I waited in the next aisle for him while picking out some vanilla pudding. When our eyes met he flashed me a grin. When he stood next to me he whispered against my ear, "Was that just for my ego's benefit, or are you suddenly predicting the future?"

I looked at him with innocence. "Both?"

He laughed out loud. We made our way through the aisles picking up random things to eat and conversing

118

comfortably along the way. He was trying to be funny and I was trying to not be amused. It was hard. He made me laugh. A lot. After the cart was almost brimming we made a beeline for the checkout. We packed up our grub and I headed out into the cold at a fast pace. We packed his trunk and I hopped inside while he returned the cart. I shivered violently. It seemed like we had skipped right over fall this year and were falling headfirst into winter. We went from 70 and sunny to 40 and chilly in just a few days. My nose was red and my teeth chattered. Not so badass looking.

He hopped in and started the heat right away. Luckily the old boat had a cranking heat system and warm air was blowing against my face in a matter of minutes. We drove back in a peaceful silence and unloaded his car practically running from the car to his apartment building. I ran into the elevator with my large bags and waited for him while cuddling into a corner. He shuffled in balancing as many bags as me and when the door finally closed he huffed so loudly with irritation that I busted out in laughter. He looked over at me in surprise and smiled. My stomach fluttered and when the elevator dinged we shuffled out and down the hall to his place. He pushed the door closed behind us and we dropped the bags on the countertop. I looked at him over the bags. He watched me. My stomach grumbled. I tried to keep a straight face, but he started laughing and it was harder. I put my hands on my hips and glared at him. He laughed louder. I started emptying the bags without a word. He chuckled. We unloaded all the bags onto the counter and he started putting things away. When most of it was gone, and he continued to look at me and chuckle, I rolled my eyes. They landed on the can of whipped cream and bottle of chocolate syrup. I snagged them and broke the seal on the cream. Just as he was turning around I tilted my head up and sprayed it into my mouth. He froze and I swallowed licking my lips. I started backing down the hallway while he stood watching me. "You got a sweet tooth, Rockstar?"

His feet started in my direction. "Getting sweeter by the minute."

I smiled and backed into the room. I didn't have to wait long for him to join me.

Chapter 8

It was strange for me. This relationship. I cringed. I wasn't even fond of calling it that. Mostly I just avoided talking about it at all. He noticed and didn't mention it either. I was getting comfortable and it worried me. I spent nearly every day there hanging out with Chase. I didn't even go home once for a week straight. We spent a great deal of time in his bedroom, and of course he made me food, and we would end up back in his bedroom. I informed him several times that my super awesomeness burned off fuel in a very short amount of time. He attempted to better my video game skills to no avail. Then he asked me to show him some of my moves. So we spent a few hours playing teacher and student which turned into a wrestling match, which turned into hot sex on the living room floor. He managed to snap a picture or two of me sleeping as well as one while I was sitting on the couch combing my hair. So far I hadn't seen any of them.

I also told him about my promise to the man in the liquor store and he didn't seem interested. His eyes lit up like flames at first then he seemed to change his mind instantly. He just mumbled something about sharing and changed the subject. We talked a lot, about him and his job. If the conversation leaned toward me I was quick to swing it back away.

He even took me with him to his friend's Halloween party. Several of his friends recognized me, not that I could blame them. I refused to actually dress up, and just wore my leather pants and jacket. They didn't seem to mind though. Chase pulled out his leathers as well and we were a hot matching set. It was a good night, but I managed to limit myself to two bottles much to his friends' disappointment. We took several rides on my bike into November. It was colder than shit, but we layered up and pushed through. I hated to park it for the winter and always managed to hold out until the snow stuck to the streets. My body started to hum with restlessness and I knew I needed to go scum hunting. I started to get snippy and cranky with Chase.

One night I told him that I needed to go out and by the time I got to the living room he was standing there waiting for me jacket in hand. We argued for a whole ten minutes before I gave up and let him come. We dropped down in an alley on the main street and my nose instantly burned with the rotting smell of demon and blood. Needless to say, we didn't have to walk far to come across a scumbag demon beating the crap out of a cop. The guy was almost unconscious and the demon continued to hit him just to watch him bleed. I pushed Chase into the shadows and taught the slimebag a lesson. When he was nothing but pulverized ash, Chase called the emergency line to let them know there was an injured cop. We disappeared just as the red and blue lights swung around the corner. We had two more run-ins that night, me letting my adrenaline out on piece of shit undead and Chase standing in the shadows watching my back. The evening out managed to cool my jets for a few days and we carried on with our... thing.

I even let him sleep in my bed a few times which were a big deal for me. In all my years as a Lost One, I had never let anyone into my house, or into my own bed. He seemed smug when I shared that detail with him.

When Thanksgiving was just around the corner, he asked me to meet his uncle. Red flags flew up all over the place and I managed to avoid the question for a few days. It was actually the morning of the holiday when he managed to sideswipe me again with the question. I had just woken up to the sunrise in his room. The orange rays warmed my cheeks even as the cold wind blew against the windows. A light snow gently pattered against the glass and I shivered. He stirred beside me and wrapped his warm body around me. I sighed. It was a really nice feeling. Unfortunately, it was a feeling that I was getting used to. Like curling up against him in my sleep used to. Like, not sure if I could actually fall asleep by myself without him next to me, used to. Like starting to feel like I was actually in a serious ... thing. I sighed again. His fingers caressed the feather tip ridges on my back and my wings stretched out towards him. He wrapped his arms around my waist and dug his nose into my hair and down my spine inhaling and gently kissing down my back. I smiled into the pillow. My muscles all relaxed just before I felt him tense against me.

"My uncle is having a dinner tonight, will you go with me?"

He held his breath waiting for my answer. I cringed. I knew it was important to him, just like he knew that it was difficult for me. "What did you tell him?"

His fingers stroked my wings again. My muscles slowly relaxed.

"Told him that I would be there and that I might bring a friend."

"You don't think he will freak when you show up with a 'smoking hot-definitely not human-but who gives a shit-badass babe'?"

I felt his lips curl up against my skin. "Are you kidding? He'd be there cheering me on."

I smiled against the pillow again. I thought for a moment. It was just an uncle, not like I was looking for permission to basically live with and have great sex with his nephew. Yet, he had said several times that he was closer to him than his parents. So it was kinda like going home to meet his dad, only not his dad. I took a deep breath and tried to pull up my badass big girl pants and suck it up. I turned my head back toward him and I raised a brow. "Nothing weird?"

He paused. "Describe weird."

I groaned.

124

He flipped me over so he was leaning over me. "You'll love him." He smiled. "I told you he's crazy, but he is awesome."

I watched him for a moment. This was a big step. This entire time I had been avoiding anything that made what we had official. Made me officially insane for getting so involved with a human. He waited patiently watching my face. I looked into those dreamy eyes and felt myself slide. "Shit."

He smiled and dropped on top of me kissing my face wildly. I giggled. He froze and watched me for a moment with surprise. Crap. There goes my rep. He smiled again and took my lips feverishly with his own. I wrapped my arms around his neck while my wings draped over his body, and we both lost ourselves in each other.

Sometime later, I watched him across the living room warily. He had pulled out his camera again, and I was curious to see what he was capturing on film. I still had yet to see the photos that he had taken recently and for whatever reason he refused to show me. So now I had to watch him when he pulled it out to make sure he wasn't taking photos of me sleeping like a baby or day dreaming about who knows what. Those kind of pictures could get me killed. If anyone saw that I had that side of me, they would see a weakness. The snow still pattered lightly against the windows as I sat on my bike in his living room. I swung my feet gently back and forth while watching him from the corner of my eye. "Looks like the last day for a bike ride."

He walked to me and tipped my chin up toward him. "Poor Angel, have to pack it away for the winter."

I scowled at him. "Only while it snows."

"Months."

I swung my leg over the handlebars so I faced him riding side saddle. "Bet me." I looked into his eyes.

"You who was freezing halfway through October wants to ride her bike into January."

"Depends on the weather."

"Snow."

"Not always."

"Until March."

"Shut up, Rockstar."

"Sorry, Angel, truth hurts."

I scowled again. Then I bit my lip. Winter was harsh on me. I hated being cold, and I hated not being able to ride my bike. I usually went on an all out hunting spree all winter long to calm my anxious nerves and to, of course, uphold my blackened diamond studded reputation. He leaned down and kissed my lip where I

126

held it prisoner between my teeth. I smiled. He was good at distracting me. He grabbed my leg and swung it over the back of my bike so I sat backwards. Then he yanked my body down until I was nearly sitting on the brake light. He leaned over me and slowly pushed me down so that I was laying on the seat. My head rested on the speedometer and my wings fell to the sides draping along the floor by the tires. I grabbed the handlebar with one hand and rested the other on my stomach. He backed away slowly. "Don't move," he whispered. I turned my head to watch him as he ran across the room to grab his camera. I rolled my eyes but didn't move. I heard several clicks and after a moment I closed my eyes. The guy still needed to make a living I suppose.

I let him drive. Even though it was my last day to enjoy it, he knew where he was going and it gave me a shield to hide behind. Blocked some of the wind. He didn't seem to mind. Just smiled and shook his head at me. The trick was getting out of the elevator without anyone noticing. Each time we were going in, we had been lucky to find the lobby deserted. At noon on Thanksgiving, I didn't think we would be as lucky. So I went out and dropped down from the balcony. I walked in the front door with my wings dragging behind me. I went to the front desk and waited until every eye was on me. The man behind the desk stood up straight and gave me his full attention. "Can I help you?"

I plastered on my sexy smile and lightened my voice. "Hi, I'm actually late for a photo shoot. As you can probably see," I reached around and tapped my wings letting them dully nudge from side to side. "Could you tell me where I can find a Mr. Chazz?"

"Mr. Chazz?" He scrambled around behind the desk looking at his paperwork.

I heard the elevator dinging as it slowly came down. "Please hurry, I am very late and these things are very heavy."

"I'm sorry Miss, I cannot seem to find any record of a Chazz renting here."

"Oh, dear!" I looked around the room. The people there were watching me and slowly getting closer. "Do any of you know where I can find him?"

They all leaped towards me eager to lend their assistance.

"Do you know his first name?"

"Are you sure you have the right apartment building?"

"Are you Biker Angel?"

"Can I have an autograph?"

The elevator dinged and I pretended to be overwhelmed and fell backward into the desk. The roar of concern filled the room as everyone reached out to me to help me up. I saw through their legs as two tires quietly moved across the floor behind them.

"Are you alright, Miss?"

"Shall I call the emergency line?"

I accepted two arms to help me up and fanned my face. "Goodness, I am sorry. Must be this extra weight I have been carrying around all morning. Anyway," I gently brushed off the helping hands. "Is this not building 2679?"

I could have sworn that was what the man said."

There was an overwhelming sigh of understanding.

"No Miss, this is 2678, you need the next building down."

"Oh! How silly of me! I'm so sorry to have bothered you all!"

"No bother at all, Miss!"

I turned away from them with a wave and a thanks, and they all waved back whispering, "Nice girl."

I scowled when I was outside in the windy cold. Chase sat there at the curb with my bike warming beneath him. He smiled at me while my wings drew into my back. "Nice show Angel. Can I see the rerun?"

I swung on behind him. "Puh-lease you get to see the main event."

He considered, then nodded his agreement. "True, I much prefer that."

I wrapped my arms around him and buried my face into his jacket. He merged into traffic and we were off.

It took no time at all. In fact, it was such a short trip that I was surprised I hadn't met this uncle sooner. Surprised that we hadn't just bumped into him on the street. Chase pulled my bike up a short drive past a few cars in front of a tall and skinny house that looked like it was squeezed in between the other ten tall and skinny houses on the street. He punched a code into a keypad on the wall and the garage door opened up. He pulled my bike up beside a nice SteelWing in jet black with shiny chrome. The poor thing looked like it had already been stored for the winter. I wanted to reach out and pat it with comfort, but the rule of the biker is to only look and not touch. Chase rolled his eyes at me when I looked at it with sadness. He grabbed my hand and pulled me toward a door.

I felt like I got hit with deja-vu. We walked into a living room of black and gray with random objects of color that stood out vibrantly. Black leather couch, gray carpet and ruby red rugs. Royal blue stereo system, and chrome framed photos on the walls. Two TV's against opposite walls and an x-box hooked up to one with the controllers sitting on the floor in front of it. After

I looked around I raised my brow at Chase and crossed my arms.

He looked at me and I whispered, "Weird!"

He shrugged and laughed pulling me behind him into another room. I heard pots and pans moving around in the kitchen as well as a few voices talking. When we rounded the corner Chase was instantly pulled into several hugs.

"Chase, glad you made it!" I recognized this voice.

"Brain. How long have you guys been here?"

"Mandy and I just got here. She ran off to help your uncle in the kitchen."

Chase chuckled, "I'm sure he needs it."

"Yeah, she ran off as soon as we walked in mumbling something about not wanting everyone to die from food poisoning tonight."

Chase laughed and reached for my hand. "You remember Angel. Angel, Brain, aka Tom."

I smiled at him and found myself in a bear hug. "Course I remember this one." He smiled at me. "Came to the party, sucks at video games but can kick ass in real life." He whispered. "At least until she hits four bottles and twenty beers, then it's all downhill."

I grinned when Chase laughed again. Brain patted him on the shoulder and got out of the way when more people came to greet Chase. They all hugged him and then hugged me. It was awkward at first, but then I started to get used to it. Chase introduced me as Angel, not Titan which was interesting. I knew he hated the name Titan or any other nickname I had for that matter. But I was glad he kept my true name to himself. After we had seen everyone in the dining room he grabbed my hand and pulled me toward the kitchen. My stomach did a little flop as we went through the doorway and into utter mayhem. A tall man stood by the oven in dark blue jeans and a black cotton shirt with a ridiculously ugly turkey apron on. He was currently glaring at a small blonde woman with her hands on her hips. When we walked in they both looked over. His eyes instantly latched onto me and I held my breath. Electric blue eyes, jet black hair with gray streaks on each side and a deadly serious expression. Shit.

The woman got a quick glance at me and instantly went to Chase. She gave him a quick hug then stood back and put her hands on her hips.

"Chase, tell Uncle to let me look in the oven."

Chase opened his mouth but did not get a word in before she started again.

"I just want to look at it, heaven knows what will happen if we leave him solely responsible for that turkey. Last year he almost fried it to a crisp!"

This broke his uncle's concentration on me and he rounded the island to stand beside her.

"What a ridiculous thing to say. Last year I simply wanted it a bit darker, and you ran around the county telling everyone that I burnt it. It tasted wonderful!"

She rolled her eyes at him. "It tasted good because Chase whipped up some kind of sauce to cover it and mask the burnt taste."

He crossed his arms over his chest. "My kitchen, my rules."

She faced him and crossed her arms, "My stomach."

I stood frozen completely unsure what to do or say, but Chase just laughed.

They both turned to him with surprise.

"Uncle, let Mandy help. It is a lot of food to handle at one time. Mandy, relax."

They both stared at him with shock and he pulled me up beside him. Their eyes fell on me and I was suddenly very self-conscious. I wore my usual attire, blue jeans black top and leather jacket. My hair was down as usual and I needed no makeup, my face was flawless. Angel of light thing. I smiled.

"Uncle, Mandy, this is Angel. Be nice." He turned back to me. "Angel, this is my Uncle Josh and Brain's fiancé Mandy."

Mandy watched me for a moment with her eyes traveling from Chase's smile and back to me. She smiled and stepped forward with a hug.

"Nice to meet you, darling. I do hope you torture him endlessly." She nodded in Chase's direction then gave Chase another hug. "Happy Thanksgiving, Chase." She whispered something in his ear and patted him on the shoulder. She gave Uncle Josh the stink eye. "I will be back in five minutes."

Uncle Josh stuck his tongue out at her retrieving back.

"Uncle."

"Chase." He stepped over and enveloped him in a tight hug. "Haven't seen you in a few weeks." His eyes fell to me like I was the one to blame.

"Just been busy."

"Yes, I can see why." His eyes traveled from my head to my toes and back again. "The famous Biker Angel in my house." He twisted his gaze back to Chase. "You couldn't come up with a better name?"

I smiled broadly and Chase sighed. They watched each other for a moment and I felt awkward again. "Where is the bathroom?"

Chase turned to me with a 'scaredy cat' expression and nodded back the way we came. "By the living room, to the left of the video games."

"Thanks." I nodded to his Uncle and quietly left the room.

I didn't listen to see what they whispered about I just quietly snuck through the loud dining room and toward the bathroom. I shut myself in and took a deep breath. Why was this so hard for me? I was the Titanium Angel and meeting Chase's uncle had my mouth shut like an obedient schoolgirl. Oh how the mighty fall. I looked in the mirror. I looked like my normal badass Lost One self. My eyes might have glowed a little warmer these days and my cheeks might have flushed a little pinker but I was still the same person. I scoffed. Who was I kidding? Chase had turned my world upside down. My entire perspective had changed. Before Chase, I had lived day by day knowing that I would eventually die. Whether a demon finally finished me off or an angel finally terminated me, I knew that me being a Forgotten; the mentally unbalanced and wild race, someday I would be killed. Before Chase, I had been ok with that. I had played the game, running, hiding and making my own rules. Acting how I wanted and never getting caught. I sighed. Now? I wanted to live. I wanted to survive, and I had something to live for. Love. My head spun and I sat on the toilet and put my head between my knees. I had gone and fallen in love, with a human. With Chase. He made me smile. He made me laugh. It lightened my heart when I heard him laugh. He melted me when he smiled. He controlled me when he touched me. My wings twitched against my skin thinking of his caress. I took a deep breath and I stood. I looked in the mirror and saw myself only this time I saw a person. I did not see someone that was lost, I saw someone with a purpose. Chase. Standing in that bathroom, I realized that not only was I head over heels in love with the guy, I would do anything to protect him. I smiled. And no one, not even the Uncle that was close to him like a father was going to change that. I straightened my shoulders and left my hiding space. A few people had left the dining room to play some video games. They looked up and smiled when I went past. I smiled back.

Brain called to me, "Hey Angel, how 'bout a rematch after dinner?"

I grinned. We both knew I sucked at video games, "You're on."

He cheered and a few people laughed.

I went into the dining room and Mandy was standing there waiting for me.

She smiled. "Hey, you alright?"

"Yes, I'm fine."

"Good." She studied me. "Don't let Uncle pull the welcome mat from under your feet. He really is a good guy, just a little stubborn sometimes when it comes to Chase and his girlfriends."

I started. "I'm not a girlfrie..."

She cut me off. "Sure you're not."

I paused. "Girlfriends?" I emphasized the s.

She smiled at me. "Not to worry, I have only ever met two and I have been friends with Chase for about six years now. First one didn't last a week, second lasted about two years and broke his heart."

Anger flooded me. Someone hurt Chase. I looked at her asking for more information. She grabbed my hand and dragged me to a quiet corner. We both leaned casually against the wall while she talked.

"After he met her he fell for her within a week. Chase is like that, opens up too easily. Cares too much too fast. Don't get me wrong, it's not a bad thing, just gets him hurt." I nodded. He had carried me home like a injured animal to tend to my wounds. She continued. "None of his friends cared for her. She was needy, self-centered and frankly a bitch. He didn't see her that way. Not until his accident." I concentrated. He had been in a motorcycle accident, been pretty hurt too. "Her true colors came out at the hospital. His Uncle told him that the bike had been totaled and that his parents were angry. She went off the deep end. Basically told him that he was worthless. That he had fucked up his bike, fucked up the income from his rich parents, and that he was never going to get anywhere with his photography. All he had was a mediocre uncle and a lame bunch of friends. She trampled him when he was already laying there broken. That was last year, and he really hasn't been the same since." She paused and looked at me. "Until now."

I looked at her with surprise. "What do you mean?"

"When you guys walked in and he laughed," she smiled. "I haven't heard him laugh that freely in almost three years. She never made him that happy. Then after she was gone, he was nothing but gray." She continued to study me. "Tom told me that Chase had met someone, told me that he was seeing a better, happier Chase. I didn't believe him until now."

I smiled and looked her in the eye. "I'm glad. He deserves to be happy."

She smiled back, "Yes, he does. Don't let Uncle put you down, he's just looking out for Chase."

A crash came from the kitchen and we both looked up. We looked at each other and made a beeline toward the commotion.

I walked in behind Mandy and Chase was standing by the stove stirring something while his Uncle started chopping something on the island. Looked like he was making a salad. He watched Mandy come in and followed her with his eyes to the oven. When she asked Chase about the turkey he rolled his eyes until they landed on me.

"Here." He tossed a knife in my direction. "Make yourself useful and cut some vegetables." I caught the knife without flinching and stepped forward. I set it on the counter and went to the sink to wash my hands. I knew Chase watched me from the corner of his eye. It was just vegetables, I could do this. I returned to the island and stood waiting. He tossed me a green pepper. I caught it and sliced it up into nice pieces. As soon as it was finished I had a red pepper tossed at me. Took care of that one. Cucumber, sliced. Celery, cut. Carrots, slivered. After about fifteen minutes and having every vegetable in the kitchen tossed at me, I had an enormous pile of cut vegetables beside me. Mandy turned and saw them and took the knife from me.

"Well, I think that is enough veggies."

"Good," Uncle Josh broke in. "She can make the potatoes."

I paused. He tossed two ten pound bags of potatoes in front of me with a grin. I didn't move. Chase noticed my distress and came over. He put an arm around my shoulders, "Don't worry, I'll help you." I smiled at him.

"What does she need help for? Don't know how to make some damn taters? What the hell is a woman good for if she can't cook?"

Chase smiled at him while my temper rose.

Mandy glared at him. "Sometimes it's better if some people don't cook."

He scoffed at her. "Have no idea what you're talking about. I make excellent food."

Chase coughed and Mandy choked. Maybe this was why Chase was so good with food, because his uncle apparently was not.

Chase grabbed two peelers from a drawer and handed me one. He pulled a trash can from under the counter and set it between two stools. He sat in one and nodded for me to sit in the other. I sat and watched him grab a potato and peel it while the peels fell into the trash can and the clean potato was thrown into a pot. I grabbed one and finished it by the time he got through six. He didn't comment, just smiled at me. His uncle scoffed continuously, but I managed to ignore him. After another fifteen minutes, they were all peeled and needed to be cut. I smiled, this I could do. I grabbed my knife from earlier and after he rinsed them I chopped them into pieces and Mandy threw them back in the pot with water to boil. His uncle stayed quiet most of the time only making snide comments in my direction every once in a while. Chase and Mandy ignored him and chatted happily to each other while I sat quietly. I only talked when they directed the conversation to me, and that was fine with me. I didn't have too much to talk about. At one point, Chase mentioned a postcard from his parents when Mandy asked him about them. When conversation slowed she asked me about my family.

"What about you Angel? Do you spend time with your family for the holidays?"

Chase froze. His uncle watched this reaction carefully. I smiled at her. "No, I'm afraid not."

"Oh, they don't like the holidays?"

"Loved them actually." My mind wandered and I rested my elbow on the table with my chin on my fist. "My mother used to sing us Christmas carols before bed at night."

Chase still sat frozen. His uncle still watched him carefully.

"Loved?"

"Yes." My eyes came back into focus when I blinked. "Lost them all several years ago."

The three of them watched me. She whispered, "All?"

I nodded with a sudden lump in my throat. "My parents and three younger brothers."

141

She starred at me in shock and her mouth opened to ask more questions, but Chase shook his head at her. She stuttered. "I'm so s-sorry."

I smiled and nodded. Chase's hand found mine and I squeezed his gently.

We carried on in a quiet but smooth silence. Uncle Josh watched me beneath his lashes, but I ignored him. Eventually dinner was ready and I had to admit, I was very hungry. Mandy and Chase managed to make sure all the food turned out well except for a minor mishap with the rolls. They turned out a little browner than desired. When we were all seated at the table, Chase to my left and Mandy to my right, his Uncle said a few words then everyone greedily dug in. Chase piled my plate high for me and his uncle scowled. I heard him mumble under his breath, "Can't even get her own food."

I straightened my shoulders and gave Chase a warm smile. He knew I had heard it and I didn't want him to think it bothered me. He smiled back and turned and gave a stern look to his uncle. Uncle Josh ignored him. Everyone talked animatedly through dinner. I loved to hear the happy chatter. It reminded me of life before my change. They all smiled and laughed and simply enjoyed each other's company. I managed to forget his Uncle and his obvious dislike of me. All of Chase's friends pulled me into their conversations and even managed to make me laugh. Chase enjoyed himself too, and after what Mandy told me, it was a big deal. I caught everyone noticing him laugh, then they would look at me and smile. They thought that I was the reason for his happiness, and they approved. I could not say for sure if that was true, but if it was, it made me happy. If I could make Chase happy just by being with him, then I was ok with that. He did the same for me. It was a dangerous game to play, but I found myself roped into playing anyway. After dinner, I was going to offer help clean up but Mandy waved me off. Brain dragged me into the living room for our video game rematch. I watched for a bit, then they handed me the controller. It was a great deal easier being sober, but I still sucked terribly.

I lost the first game and demanded to play something easier. They laughed and put in a motorcycle race game. I rolled my eyes at them. Just because I had one in real life didn't mean I could manage one on a screen better. I came in eighth place on my first try and fourth on my second try. Brain just smiled while giving me pointers. Another guy named Jack, whom I recognized from Chase's apartment, played against me next. He told me he was just as bad so maybe I had a better chance of winning. I shrugged out of my jacket while everyone sat around the TV to watch. Chase, Mandy, and Uncle Josh were still in the kitchen. I could hear them talking through the dining room, but I blocked them out. I didn't feel like eavesdropping on his argument with his uncle. I focused on the game and made third place, then in the next round I got a flat tire and came in seventh. Everyone booed when my score came up and I laughed.

143

I felt my wings tickle against my skin and heard another scoff behind me and everyone turned to find Chase, Mandy and his uncle standing back watching. Chase was angry, I could tell right away. Mandy was unhappy and looked uncomfortably in the middle. His uncle crossed his arms.

"Well, Angel. You can't cook, can't clean up, and obviously can't play games. The fact that you are not human denies you any chance of ever having a real relationship. What exactly are you good for, besides the obvious?" He gestures to me. I look down at myself. I wore tight fitting blue jeans and a skimpy black shirt. My hips jutted out provocatively and I had a little too much cleavage showing. I couldn't really help that, it was hard to find shirts that left my shoulder blades bare. It only took a second for me to understand his meaning. He obviously thought that the only thing I was good for was sex, like a common slut. My eyes burned. Chase grabbed his Uncle's arm angrily, but he shook him off. The room was silent as everyone stared in shock. He just looked at me, waiting. I handed the controller to whoever was next to me, and slowly walked toward him.

I should have kicked his ass right then and there. I would have if Chase wasn't so important to me. I would have picked him up by the shirt and slammed him into the wall. No one who knew me, would dare insult me and think to live afterwards. Chase tried to step between us but I silently shook my head at him.

He backed away. Mandy walked around me to join Brain. His uncle raised a brow.

I got up close and in his face. I had to look up a little because he had a good foot on me, but it didn't make me any less dangerous. "Do you and I need to go to another room and have a nice talk?"

He smiled at me. "No, Angel." He spit out my name like it was distasteful in his mouth. "We can talk right here."

I snapped. I was trying to be nice. To save our audience from a little show. He was being ridiculous, and upsetting Chase. It pissed me off. I grabbed him by the shirt and pulled his face down to my level. He was surprised.

"Last chance."

"Sorry, Angel. You're not my type."

My arm reacted before my brain did. One second he was in front of me the next he was flipping over my head and landing flat on his back.

A gasp sounded across the room. His uncle lay stunned. I froze for a second and bit my lip looking at Chase. Oh shit, did I really just do that? His eyes met mine and he was just as surprised as me. He saw my face and he burst out laughing. Every head turned to him. He bent over with his hands on his knees, laughter filling the silent room. I turned to his uncle who watched Chase with amazement. The others slowly began to join Chase in laughter. I reached down and grabbed Uncle Josh's shirt again and pulled him up. When he stood, I pointed to the garage and walked around him. I went through the door and went to sit on my bike, waiting.

It didn't take long for him to follow. I didn't think it would. I was surprised though that Chase didn't follow as well.

He walked in and shut the door behind him. His eyes widened when they landed on the bike, but he crossed his arms and leaned against the door.

"So are we gonna play around here or are you gonna tell me what your problem is?" I watched him.

"You are my problem, Angel."

"I get that, my question is why?"

"You're not good enough for him."

I smiled. "And this is your decision?"

"Oh, it's not up to me. But I'll be damned if I sit by and keep my mouth shut."

"So," I watched him. "You have known me for an entire four hours now. And based off what exactly are you basing this opinion of yours?" He opened his mouth to speak and I cut him off. "And if you tell me

146

it's because I can't cook or play video games, I just might shoot you and be done with it."

He stared at me. "You are not normal."

I laughed out loud, "And who is?"

"You're not human."

"Wow, got that already did you?"

"I don't like your kind."

This surprised me. "And just what kind do you think that I am?"

"Light Angel."

"Wrong," I said it so quickly and he looked at me with surprise.

"I saw your back, your looks, and your strength. Don't play me like a fool."

"I am not a Light Angel."

"Then what the hell are you?"

"Nothing you ever came across before. So what's with the hatred for Angels?"

His face blanched. "They are all bad news. They ruin lives and don't look back."

I studied him. I saw in his eyes, something hurt, something broken. I whispered, "Someone broke your heart."

His shoulders sagged a bit. "No. An angel pulverized it. And I won't let you do the same to my nephew. And don't try to deny it, it is what you will do. It may not be today or tomorrow, but someday you will break him."

A lump caught in my throat. Perhaps somehow, I had already known this. Yet, when he said it, it became real. I let my wall of attitude down and looked at him. I needed to know because this is something that actually scared me. "What happened to you?"

He pushed off the wall and sat on a stool. He rubbed his face and he took a deep breath. Then he raced into the story trying not to get caught in the memories. "I was his age, mid twenties, full of life, ready to take on the world. Just like him. I ran into a beautiful young thing one night in a diner. Beautiful golden hair and pale white skin with the bluest eyes. She was sitting all by herself and quiet but when she smiled you saw stars. We ended up talking then we saw each other again, then we started making plans to see each other all the time. Within a few months I was head over heels for her, she was the light in my darkness, the warmth in the coldness. She was everything to me. I told her how I felt and she told me that she had to tell me something about herself. She showed me her wings that night. Beautiful white wings. They were feather soft and graceful. Strong and warm. I loved them and she was thrilled and relieved at the same time. For some reason she had thought that I would hate them, hate her because of them. She told me after that, that she loved me, that she wanted to spend our lives together. I actually believed her."

I watched the pain skitter across his face as memories resurfaced.

"She actually stuck around for about five years. Told me all about the world and the dangers that lurked around every corner. She of course had her job doing what angels do, and I worked in a garage down the street. So when things happened, she often told me about it. It was when my younger sister had Chase, that I started seeing a different side to my angel. I told her one day that I wanted children, and she freaked. Went on a rampage about her never being able to have children because she was an angel. Told me that she could never have kids, could never be a mother, would never even age. That I would get older and older and die and she would still be stuck in the same place. I told her that I was okay not having kids, that I would have a nephew to spoil. I told her that I would still love her in sixty years and that she would always be the center of my world. She settled, but after that she was different. She slowly distanced herself. It was almost fifteen long years of me blinding myself to the hollowness we were making. Eventually, she was gone for weeks at a time working and I was never home because I was always hanging out with Chase while my sister and her husband worked. Almost ten years ago, she came home in tears. Told me that she had messed up bad, lost someone she was supposed to watch. Someone extremely dangerous and extremely important. The higher powers were extremely angry with her and unsure how to punish her. I told her we could run. We could go into hiding. I could get a better job and she could stay safely at home. She laughed at me. Wanted to know why I still dreamed of happily ever after. Told me that I was already in my forties and she was still practically a teenager. She told me that I didn't make enough money and I would probably be dead in ten years, so she probably shouldn't waste any more time on me. She walked out and never looked back."

I was silent for a moment. "What was her name?"

He was lost in his memories. "Meredith."

My own memories struggled to the surface. He shook his head to clear his thoughts. Then he looked at me. "I don't know you, I have no intention of getting to know you. Angel or not, I don't want the same thing to happen to Chase."

"It won't," I said this to both of us for reassurance.

"How do you know?"

"I'm different."

"What exactly are you?"

150

I smiled. "I'm the extremely important person your girlfriend lost ten years ago."

Chapter 9

My shoulders relaxed slightly when the door shut behind us. I immediately started my bike and swung my leg over sitting on the soft leather. Chase pulled his jacket over his shoulders and zipped it up tight. I slid back as he pulled his gloves on. He raised a brow at me. "Your place or mine Angel?"

I considered. I hadn't been home for more than five minutes in a few days."Mine."

He nodded and pushed a button on the SteelWing making the garage door lift. He sat in front of me and pulled my bike out stopping to punch the code into the keypad making it close again. The wind was bitter and a light snow sprinkled the earth. The dark roads were wet but so far clear. After a few minutes down the road, I felt Chase shiver against me between the shaking of my arms and my chattering teeth. I reached back and unzipped the zipper against my spine halfway, allowing freedom for my wings. They shivered once against the chill and I slowly wrapped them around us like a shield. I instantly felt better and Chase stopped shivering. We made it to my place within twenty minutes and after a quick scan of my property I pushed the button for my garage door and we glided into the warmth.

He parked it and we both sat not moving. My wings still curled around him and my arms hung tightly around his waist. He leaned back into me pulling me closer. My wings tightened around us and I sighed. It was a quiet few moments of peace and warmth. When I started to feel my eyes droop I loosened my grip and stood.

I knew Chase wanted to know what had happened with his uncle. We had after all returned quietly from the garage within twenty minutes and after that he had been civil to me. He still disliked me, out of fear. Fear for Chase. But he had loosened up a little after our talk. Chase and I enjoyed the rest of the evening and had been first to leave the party crowd. His uncle had hugged Chase tightly and nodded once to me. He had already warned me. Chase was his only nephew, and I was responsible if anything happened to him.

So now we sat in front of the fireplace, me sitting in front of him and leaning back against him. He had one arm propping him up and the other around me.

After about ten minutes, he sighed. "Are you going to tell me what you talked about?"

"Nope."

"He is my uncle, and I think I should know why of all the people in the world, he dislikes the one person that I thought he would love."

"He has a thing against angels. No big deal."

153

"Really?"

"Some chick walked all over him."

He paused. "Who?"

"Meredith."

"Meredith was an angel?"

"Apparently."

"Wow."

I smiled. "Just wow?"

"Never saw that coming."

"Apparently it was the going that was the issue."

"Spill."

"Nope, his business, not mine."

He sighed and it was quiet for a few more minutes.

"You really need some color in this room."

"Why?"

"It's boring."

"I'm in it."

He smiled against my neck. "Much as I know you enhance the room, you need something else. Like furniture, or Christmas decorations. For someone that loves Christmas music as much as you, you need some Christmas color in your house."

I sighed. "Whatever."

"So," he started. "Three younger brothers?"

"Yup." I closed my eyes and let my wings curl around us.

"You must have been very busy."

"Always. They were good kids."

"Anything like you, I can believe it."

I scoffed. "Whatever."

He paused as I ended the conversation. His fingers stroked my wings. They stretched beneath his touch and gently settled against him.

"Random question, what is the difference between dark wings and light wings? Is it really just good and evil?"

I chuckled. "You humans, so basic." He was quiet, waiting. I sighed. "It isn't really good or evil, more like what an angel holds inside them. Light Angels are typically peaceful. They are happy, content, caring, emotionally stable and alive. Their wings reflect that. Bright, light and soft. Dark Angels can be angry or sad. They can feel like they are missing great pieces of themselves. They can be mentally unstable or emotionally distraught. They are darkening because their life is decaying, they are not really living. Their wings are dark, heavy and greasy."

I twisted to look at him, to see if he understood what I was saying. He seemed to be pondering my words.

"So, you're saying that the only difference between the two is that for one reason or another, some fall apart or start to lose themselves, start to die and that is what makes them Dark."

I nodded. "The equator. Some fall up, and some fall down."

"And you are still in the middle, with me."

I closed my eyes relaxing against him as he continued stroking my wings. "With you."

I fell asleep there in his arms and I woke up in my bed to the sound of his phone vibrating. I peeked through my eyelids as his arm stretched over to grab the irritating device off my empty nightstand. I watched him read the screen then toss the phone back on the table. He turned back to me snuggling against me. I smiled.

"Who was that?"

"Brain."

I waited. He smiled. "He wants to meet at the Blue Room on Saturday to celebrate."

Again I waited. I didn't even have to ask.

"My birthday."

I smiled. "Your birthday is Saturday?"

"Actually it's Friday. The big 2-8."

I smiled. "Never thought I would date a man almost a decade my senior."

"Hey! You're not that much younger."

"Sorry, Rockstar, I will be nineteen for a very long time."

"You don't look nineteen."

"Never did." I grinned.

"You up for going?"

I thought about it. I would be fine so long as Billy didn't cause a scene. Only one way to find out. "Sure."

I stood up and he grumbled. "Where are you headed?"

I turned back to face him. "I am dropping you off then I have to run somewhere."

He opened his mouth, but I stopped him. "No, Rockstar, you cannot come with."

"Are you going to start a fight? Or get drunk? Or just do anything that might put your life in danger?"

I smiled. "Nope. No danger today."

He pouted. "Alright, I guess I can find something to do with my life today."

I grinned. "I'm sure you can."

Chapter 10

It was difficult. Pulling off the whole "silently sneaking in with hundreds of pounds of shiny metal" in my hands. It was like 2 am on the big day and I was certain Chase had stayed up most of the night waiting for me. So flying up here and quietly sneaking in was more stressful than I thought it would be. As always, the glass door was slightly left open for yours truly. I managed to get the damn thing inside and quietly pushed to the center of his living room. He had known for a few days that I was up to something, he just didn't have any idea what. I smiled as I tied a ridiculously large red bow around it and tiptoed back to his room. I stripped and crawled in beside him. He wrapped his arms around me and whispered in my ear about being late. I kissed him and made him forget all about it. When he woke shortly after dawn and stood heading for the shower, I groaned and pulled him back into bed for another hour. When he thought he was sneaking his way to the shower by tiptoeing away from me, I let him go. When I heard him get into the running water, I hopped out of bed and threw on some clothes. I tiptoed past the bathroom and sat on the couch waiting. Within ten minutes, I heard his footsteps gently padding down the short hallway. I tried to play it cool but caught myself grinning.

"What are you up to out he..." He froze when his eyes landed on the bike.

"Holy shit!" His jaw almost touched his feet and he walked over to it and just stared.

I went to him. "A Wind Runner TC, Electric blue, with stainless steel and one hell of an engine. I should know, I test drove it." He studied it, his fingers reaching out to touch the bright blue tank and flowing over the steel wings I had them add to the sides. I also had them write "Rockstar" in bold green letters across the gas tank. He turned to me in awe. His mouth opened, but nothing came out. I smiled. "Happy Birthday, Rockstar."

His face broke into a massive grin and he reached for me, picking me up and spinning me in a circle. His eyes watched my face and when he stopped he pulled me to him and kissed me hard. "You are amazing."

I rolled my eyes. "Duh."

He laughed and set me down to look at it again. Luckily by the time I got out of the shower, he had stopped drooling and was making food. I smiled when I saw grilled cheese frying on the stove.

We decided to spend the day doing something exciting. Well, non-dangerous exciting. I told him I was up for something active to burn off energy and he told me he wanted to go outside. I raised a brow at him and pointed to the snow covered balcony. He stood firm. Told me to get dressed we were going out for the day. I half expected him to stuff me in his car and drive somewhere frigid, but instead he pulled me out onto the balcony and pointed south. He winked at me and whispered in my ear about a place. I shivered and huffed and stretched my wings out. I stood behind him, wrapped my arms around his chest and my legs around his waist and headed south. I was waiting for him to point me downward after we were in the air for half an hour, but he was silent. He actually looked back at me and smiled. "Pick up the pace Angel, we are losing daylight."

I smiled back and catapulted forward, doubling my speed through the winter air. My cheeks burned a bit with the cold, but I noticed that the longer we flew the warmer it got. Looking down I noticed that the snow was disappearing being replaced by dark browns and light greens. After another twenty minutes, he pointed down. "See that small brown building?" I nodded. "We need to stop there."

I dropped instantly and he grabbed my arms tighter. We fell to the earth like deadweight until we were near enough that I needed to slow down. I slowly dropped him to his feet and jumped to mine. He gained his footing fast and took off at a brisk pace toward the building. I had to jog to keep up. We walked into John's Place and the door dinged as we passed through. A large man appeared from the back wearing an apron and a white baseball cap. He recognized Chase right away and smiled, coming around from behind the counter. He wrapped Chase in a bear hug and smacked him on the back.

"Chase, my boy what brings you out this way?"

"Hey John, just visiting for the day, need some food."

"Well, you certainly know where to come." He grinned and spotted me behind Chase. "Who's this pretty thing?"

Chase smiled and pulled me forward. "This gorgeous lady here is Angel. Angel this is John, Mandy's dad."

His eyes widened and his grin spread. "Ah, so this is Angel." He shook my hand and pulled me in for a hug. "I have heard a great deal about you, my dear." He leaned down and whispered, "Even about the little flip you gave old Josh." He winked. I cringed and Chase chuckled. He watched Chase smile then he winked at me again. "Well, what can I get you two?"

"We need a mobile lunch if it isn't too much trouble."

He waved him off. "No trouble at all. Give me ten minutes and I will have it ready for you." He twirled around and disappeared back behind the counter.

I raised a brow at Chase. "Do this often?"

"Not in awhile. Used to come this way with the bike every few weeks."

I nodded and walked around studying the random things that John had for sale. It was almost a general store meets a carry out diner kind of joint. "So where are we headed?"

"You'll see when we get there."

"Hmmm." I turned around and continued my browsing.

True to his word within ten minutes he was handing Chase a white paper bag and two water bottles. Chase handed him some money from his jean pocket and shook his hand. "Thanks, John."

"Anytime, Chase, enjoy your hike."

"Always do." He smiled and we turned.

I smiled and waved.

"Nice to meet you, Angel, hope I see you again."

We walked out and he pointed toward a hill in the distance. "We are going there. We can walk if you're tired, but it will take long..."

His words were cut off by me taking his hand and pulling him up into the air with me. We glided above the trees toward the foggy green hill that he had pointed to. After a few moments, he pointed to a small clearing halfway up the hill. When we landed, I raised my brow at the woodsy, nothing special hillside that we were looking at. He smiled at me. He grabbed my face and kissed me. "We have to walk from here to experience it." My stomach grumbled in response and he chuckled. He grabbed my hand and we started the hike up the hill that now looked like a mountain. I had no problem with the hike -- my stomach was the one that was pissed. It did not like to be kept waiting, and whatever was in that bag smelt like a five-course meal with dessert.

I was starting to wonder what could possibly be worth it when his hand squeezed mine and with a few final steps we topped the mountain and looked out into total freedom. He smiled and I froze. I had never in my life seen anything quite so beautiful as this view. I stepped forward toward the edge and took a deep breath. The air was so clean and light, it fluttered warmly against my cheeks. Beneath me, the ocean rolled and foamed wave after wave of blue-green water. Birds flew in the horizon as the sunlight glinted off their wings and glittered against the waves. The wind turned and blew against me. I smiled and let myself have a Titanic moment, raising my arms like wings and closing my eyes letting the wind blow past me. Chase stepped up behind me and wrapped his arms around me holding me tight against him. He tucked his head into my neck and kissed me gently where my blood pumped ferociously. His lips slowly heated a trail from my neck down my back along the raised ridges where my wings lay. My heart raced while my body heated and I turned back to him. He ran a hand slowly from my neck down along my spine and without any command from me, my wings fluttered out just from his touch. He smiled slyly. He must have been practicing that little trick. He kissed me gently. Then again with more heat. Then again, and again slowly building fire and passion each time. I pulled back and looked at him. "Is this where you bring all your girlfriends to get them in the mood?"

He looked at me puzzled. Then surprised. "Actually, I've never brought anyone here."

I was speechless. So I was the first person important enough to bring to his favorite spot.

Then he smiled at me. "Just so you are aware, you just called yourself my girlfriend, and you cannot take it back." My breath froze at my mistake. I bit my lip wondering how I was going to get myself out of that one when he knocked my legs out from under me and I fell in a heap to the soft grassy earth. He covered me with his body kissing me deeply and not letting me fight back. When he pulled away I opened my mouth to say something but he pulled the front of my shirt down and covered the ruby red lace tips with his mouth. Whatever I was about to say flew out and got carried away on the wind. Instead, I moaned and he settled more of his weight down on me. In no time at all he had me feverish with passion and frantic with need. He leaned down and whispered into my ear. "Admit it, Crimson, right now, right here, with me, you are where you're supposed to be." His nose rubbed mine and he watched me from above. Our eyes hooked and he smiled. "With me."

I watched the emotions swirling feverishly in his eyes. I raised my hand up to his cheek and traced his lips like I had watched him do that first night so long ago. "With you," I whispered. His eyes exploded with love and fire and his lips took mine once again. Laying together up on that hilltop overlooking the world, we both knew what was happening. We both felt it, knew the other was feeling it as well and we basked in the glory of it.

We stayed long enough to watch the sunset, after eating the delicious food that had been hiding in the mediocre white bag. My nose had been right though, five-course meal and dessert. My kind of picnic. Then we sat on that hilltop in content silence with only each other's arms to hold us down from floating into complete oblivion.

Chapter 11

I rolled over in his bed and tossed a pillow in his general direction. It was well past noon and this was the tenth time he had tried to rouse me from bed. The man had no idea how a long flight with double the weight really drained a girl. Not to mention, the whole emotional roller coaster while realizing you're in love at the top of the world, then being expected to do a return flight. I was exhausted. I moaned and crankily threw another pillow when he laughed at me. I pulled the covers up over my naked body and put the last pillow over my head. It was quiet for a moment and I thought that he had actually left me alone when the blanket started inching its way down. I groaned. The man was going to drive me insane! I took a deep breath ready to give him a swift kick in the ass but when I went to move my energy was nowhere to be found. Instead, I whined out loud. "Chase I love you to death, but if you don't let me go back to sleep, I will murder you!" He stopped. I sighed, thinking that finally I was getting blissful quiet. Then my words echoed in my head. Oh My God. I sat upright like a bolt of lightning with wide eyes wondering if he had heard me. He stood frozen at the edge of the bed staring at me with wide eyes and a gaping mouth. The blanket dropped from his grasp and the room was so silent I heard the whisper of it landing on the floor.

My heart sped and pumped crazily in my eardrums. I needed to fix this. Shit, how do I fix this? Just kidding? A silly laugh? A badass shrug of whatever? My eyes watched his as his watched mine. Instead, I sat there speechless. Unfortunately, in his eyes, it proved my guilt. As the seconds ticked by and still nothing came from my lips, his eyes slowly darkened. His lips slowly lifted on one side in that smartass twitch that I was growing too fond of. He slowly walked toward me, and my entire body went on alert. I watched his eyes and I saw the quick pounding of his heart against his smooth chest. Against his neck. My mouth went dry. I slowly inched my way back from him on the bed. Not enough to draw his attention, but enough that an escape was still possible. He was at the side now, and I inched away too quickly, his eyes snapped onto me and he stilled. I froze and my chest rose and fell too fast. His eyes fell to my nude chest and his eyes continued to burn. I counted to three and I pitched backwards somehow getting my feet under me and taking a leap away from him. He must have known what I was doing because he had already jumped across the bed in two leaps and pinned me against the wall. I couldn't breathe. He didn't even speak, his lips found mine and feasted. His breath burned like hot coals and his skin melted into me like rays of sunlight. His hand wrapped itself in my hair tightly, holding my head prisoner. He was rough, hot and wild. He kissed me like he had waited an eternity just to taste my lips and only had this one small chance. When his teeth released my lips I had to drag air into my lungs. His hands were rough and trailed fire over me, they pulled, squeezed and gently scratched my skin. I moaned loudly, the sound reverberating along the walls. My mind stopped functioning, the only thing that went through my head was how much I wanted this man, right now, and forever. My legs were spread apart and my hips lifted until my legs were wrapped around him. He shoved into me, sliding in on a wave of golden heat and pushing us both into madness. Sweat rolled down our bodies as he pushed me farther and farther toward the edge. My lips were numb and my body liquid lava. I screamed out loud to him, my head thrown back against the wall waiting for the fireworks to explode and break me into a thousand magnificent pieces. His hand grabbed my chin pulling my head back down.

"Open your eyes." He yelled at me.

I pried them open with my last bit of energy and looked into his burning ones as he continued pumping.

"Tell me." He whispered hoarsely.

They started to flutter closed as I felt the end coming closer.

He shook my chin. "Crimson! Tell me, damn it!" He yelled again.

I opened them once more and dug my nails into his back as I started to crest. His eyes never left mine. I opened my mouth and before I could stop them they tumbled out breathlessly. "I love you, Chase."

He slammed into me again and again as I shattered and he yelled out in deep satisfaction as we both fell into blissful madness.

Chapter 12

I stayed on alert as we walked into the bar. Not that I was worried, just not interested in Billy causing a scene again. I was beyond exhausted and barely able to put one foot in front of the other at this point. I had woken up just an hour ago in Chase's bed, completely and totally disoriented. I knew what had happened. I wasn't a total moron to think that that had all been a very, very nice dream. I sighed, the cat was definitely out of the bag, and it was too big of a cat to stuff in the closet, soooo I was outta luck. I had moaned and groaned through my shower and while I dressed. When I had stumbled out to find him, he had been facing away from me and I saw the scratches I had left on his back. I cringed thinking they probably hurt like a bitch, but when he felt me standing there and turned around his smile beamed so brightly I had needed to shield my eyes. He had walked right over, kissed me on the lips, and swung me up into his arms. He had carried me to the table and put me down in front of a steaming plate of mashed potatoes, gravy and grilled chicken. I had wanted to hit him for being so energetic and happy, but I was hungry, so I held back. Now, here I was following him into the bar to make sure he didn't get himself killed or hurt.

The place had been changed up a bit since last time. New tables and booths and a few new decorations on the same stupid blue walls. I smiled thinking that most everything had likely suffered water damage. Chase spotted his friends right away and pulled me by the hand towards them. I sighed with relief that I didn't see the large bulky form of Billy anywhere in the room. When we got to the table, people shook hands and hugged. I was roped into a few embraces myself. Mandy was happy to see me and glad to see Chase still smiling. I sat next to her and she decided to talk my ear off. I smiled and let her, half listening to everything she said and making an effort to give her decent responses. Chase had a good time, talking and laughing with his friends. He kept looking over at me and smiling. I couldn't help myself and smiled back. It was nice to slow down and enjoy the moment.

We actually ended up being the last to leave after Mandy and Brain. Chase was enjoying himself too much for me to cut it short because I needed sleep. So I sat back and watched him have fun. I was paying the tab when he whispered in my ear that he had to run to the restroom. I nodded. He walked up toward the stairway and under it to the restrooms. I sat waiting, yawning against my palm. My eyes closed for just a second and it was enough for me to jolt awake moments later when someone bumped into my chair. My heart raced when I realized my mistake. I looked around for Chase and didn't see him. I searched again, and still did not find him. I stood and slowly walked toward the restrooms. I got to the stairway and

172

glanced up. Billy stood there glaring down at me with his arms crossed. I was about to turn away when he crooked a finger at me and smiled. I shook my head, no way was I getting into that tonight. He just smiled again and reached behind him pulling Chase out the doorway far enough that I could see him. Far enough that I could see his split lip and pissed off expression. My eyes burned and I straightened my back and made my way up the stairs. This night had just gotten even longer.

Billy led me through the doorway and down a hall, shoving Chase ahead of him as he went. He was purposely trying to irritate me, and it was working. I wanted to cut his head off while he was walking, but I figured it would probably just get me into more trouble. We walked down to the end of the hallway and he opened the door shoving Chase inside. He took a small step back and waited. I took a deep breath, straightened up and stepped into whatever was coming next.

Now, remember how I said I thought of Demons as having three levels? it's the same with vamps. First level is the high rollers, the guys that have their shit together. Rare, but they existed because they found a system, and it worked. Second level is the guys that have an extremely small chance of ever getting their shit together. If they followed the right footsteps, they might get up to that first level, but probably not. The third level is the dumb shits. The ones that had absolutely no hope of getting anywhere and were better off just taking orders. I followed Chase into a room full of twos and threes. Billy walked very close behind me, obviously trying to put me on edge. I ignored him and went to Chase. He looked at me and mouthed the word 'sorry.' I shook my head at him, it wasn't his fault, I was the one that fell asleep. I grabbed his hand and squeezed gently for reassurance. For whom? Both of us. I looked around and shuddered. There were a lot of bloodsuckers in here. At least five level threes were standing on one side of the room looking at us like fresh meat. Some hissed and smiled, and others whistled and made kissing noises at me. I gave them the bird. The other side of the room had about five more level two guys. This is where Billy fit in. They were better dressed than the threes, but still not quite on top. They sat quietly drinking their alcohol and watching with mild interest. Billy stood behind us and crossed his arms. We were waiting, probably for the boss.

Sure enough within two minutes, the door reopened and three guys walked in. Two stage two linebackers, followed by the big gun. They wore crisp suits, with tidy white collars. Shiny black shoes and gold watches. The big gun, obviously the man in charge, let his eyes explore the room and when his gaze landed on me, his lips stretched into a wide smile. This must be Joe. He was smaller than Billy, but still packed with strength. His dark hair was slicked back and his lips so red that it looked like he had just applied candy apple red lipstick. His gaze followed me from head to toe and slowly took notice of my hand connected with

174

Chase's. He gave him a small glance then moved back to study me. I've had people look before, trust me when I say I was used to people looking to their full advantage. But this was a slow, intense inspection. Like he was deciding on a piece of steak.

I figured when his teeth pulled back into a smile and his fangs elongated outward, that he must have liked what he saw. He nodded to Billy and before I could respond, Chase was shoved away from me and into another guy's hold, while Billy pulled my arms sharply behind me making the muscles in my shoulders pull and stretch painfully. My wings bunched together uncomfortably along my skin. I watched Chase who tried his hardest to fight the vamp holding him, but he had no chance, and he eventually just hung limply from his prison watching me. Billy pushed me forward toward Joe, who had found a seat against the wall. It was like a throne, surrounded on both sides by his suits, who leaned casually behind him. Joe continued to watch me as I struggled against Billy's hold. I knew it was pointless to take Billy out. I would have just had another ten take his place. I ground my teeth together to keep my mouth shut.

Everyone stayed silent. Joe finally opened his mouth to talk. His voice was cold, smooth, and it gave me goosebumps. "Finally, the Titanium Angel has done me the pleasure of gracing my presence." Snickers came from the three's. He ignored them and continued. "I must tell you how upset I was to hear I had missed you when you visited us last, but how happy I am to see that you have returned." He watched me with his cold red eyes. "I must admit that I have been waiting several years to meet you, simply because you are the most famous and most sought after undead of the century. There is no one in the entire universe quite like you. Interesting fate you have been given, don't you think?"

"Luck," I muttered.

He laughed out loud and stood quickly. "Luck! You think luck has gotten you this far in our world?" He watched me then paced a bit."No, you don't truly believe that. I have heard many things about you, Titan. I think you make your own luck. I think you, Titanium Angel, write your own destiny." He paced a little before me. I watched him, waiting for the point to this conversation. He turned back and sat back into his throne. "You see, Lost One, I have a business proposition for you, a new direction for that destiny of yours and I do hope you consider it wisely."

I rolled my eyes. "I'm not looking for work right now, but I'll be sure to look you up when I'm in the market." My arms were yanked back further causing my back to crack. Billy kicked me in the back of the knee and my legs gave out. I fell to my knees and scowled.

Joe laughed as his eyes traveled along me again. "Oh, please hear me out, Titan. You might find my offer more interesting than you think." He stood once more as if preparing to deliver an important lecture. "You see, I have been looking for a partner, you could say. Searching everywhere really. I spent years searching in my own kind but never found someone that had what I wanted. I even looked to other races for someone with a special something that would really give me the extra zing I find myself needing. I think you met one of my possible candidates the last time you visited." I had a flash of the whiny demon hoe that had complained about waiting for her meeting with Joe. For some reason, it was funny to me that I was on a list of runners like her. I laughed out loud before I could stop it.

His eyes burned into me. "Think that is funny do you? I suppose it was a little funny when I added you to the list and all the others fell way below my standards. None of them were smart enough, strong enough, or even powerful enough compared to you." He smiled, "And let's face it, no one compares to the package that you come in my dear." A few whistles sounded from the other wall again and I glared. He looked at them and growled. "Out." In a second all of the threes were gone leaving only the twos, and us. He turned back to me.

"I could do so many great things with you by my side Titan. With your special talents and abilities, we could change the world. All the things we could do..." His eyes grew. "Join me, I'll give you anything you want, anything you desire."

I struggled while my arms started to ache, but Billy held firm. "I don't know what you're talking about. I don't have any special talents. I'm a Forgotten, nothing more than a fucked up angel."

"Nothing more?" He laughed hysterically. "Think about it, Titan!" He yelled at me in a gay rage. "You soul was lost on its path and you became a Forgotten because it stretched in different directions." He smiled at me and my heart sped. "Why ever could your soul not break into more directions than the simple two that you know of?" I froze. He laughed. "All these years you have gone thinking that you are caught somewhere between an angel of light and an angel of dark, but what if there are more doorways?" He stepped up to me and brought his face close to mine. "I know all about you, Titan. You spent the first year running and hiding on the brink of insanity. No one actually believes there is a sane bone in your body. That's one of the reasons that you scare them. They all think you're crazy, and you let them believe it. You spent two years after that calling yourself a rebel. Drinking to your heart's content and satisfying your craving for sex as often as you pleased. Now? You're off the grid, working as some kind of fucked up vigilante. Playing by your own rules and doing as you see fit." He leaned toward me to whisper. "Do you honestly think that the shadow that covers your heart is only due to your dark angel side? What if..." he backed away and his voice echoed through the room again. "What if all that rage and hate towards your enemies is coming from somewhere else? Somewhere blacker than a dark angel?" He got close again whispering near enough to my face that I could see blood stains on his teeth. My stomach rolled, and I tried to back away, but Billy grabbed my hair and held tight. "Perhaps your body's constant craving for sex and your wild and untamable heart is part demon. That fire that burns endlessly inside you, making you restless and agitated, it can't all be simply Dark Angel. Maybe the way your mind loves the hunt, the chase, and the bloodbath is not your Light Angel seeking out balance but your body's way of craving what you really need. Blood."

I snarled at him. "I'm nothing like you."

He laughed and backed away. "You have absolutely no idea what you are Titan, how could you possibly know what you need?"

Chase struggled against the guy by the door and I looked over to him. Joe watched me with interest. "Why are you with this human anyway Titan?" he looked him over and dismissed him. "He is nothing but a worthless mortal plaything. You can stay here with me Titan." He smiled at me. "You can become so much more. More power, more strength, more attention to your every need. I can give you all of that and more." He paused and looked disgusted. "I might even let you keep him as a pet."

"Not interested." Billy yanked my hair back.

"You know, I could make you stay." He wrapped a hand around my neck and pulled me up until I was standing. He leaned in close to me and slowly ran a finger from my lips to my throat. "Do you know what happens to a vampire when they drink another's blood?" He pulled back so he could watch my face. "If they take just enough, almost to the point of making the host pass out but not too much that they kill them, they create a bond. I'm not talking about that simple romantic bond people dream about in movies. A true bond that can withstand anything in the universe. A bond so strong that only death can break it. The blood would revive you, heal injuries and make you stronger, but most importantly it would create the ultimate connection." He stepped back. "If what I suspect about you Titan, is true, then a little blood would change your entire world."

"Thanks for the offer, but I think I will pass." My heart was frozen in my chest. I was so very confused, tired and if I was being honest, rattled.

He hissed and his fangs peeked through. "I could do it, Titan. I could sink my teeth into that delicious skin of yours, and then..." he laughed. "Then things could get very interesting." He followed my eyes back to Chase. "I could make you forget your human, make you think of only me, of the thought of my fangs piercing your neck while my body pierced your body." His breathing turned heavy. "I could connect with you in a way that I would know your every move, and your every feeling, until the end of time. Your everything would be mine."

I needed to get out of here. I looked up at him with a smile. "I don't suppose you would let me go home and sleep on it for a few days, or I dunno... decades?"

He watched me and his eyes turned to the pulse at my neck. "I see your heart pumping frantically Titan." He stalked closer to me. Billy held firm to his strong grip on my hair and hands. I needed to get us both out of here or things were going to go very badly. Chase struggled against the vamp holding him, but it did no good. We were both stuck with little hope of escape, surrounded as we were. He placed his fingers on my throat where the blood pumped with adrenaline. "All you have to do my beautiful Lost One, is say yes and things will run smoothly from here."

I smiled. "Not even if Hell froze over."

He stepped back and hissed at me. "Then you leave me no choice but to coerce you with force. You know as well as I that others search tirelessly for you Titan. Angels, Demons, other covens and even humans will stop at nothing until they own you. I cannot simply stand aside and let them have you." He opened his mouth wider and I saw his fangs elongate against his red lips. I heard Chase struggling again with the vampire and hoped he could somehow manage to get free. Billy still held my arms tight and when Joe was just close enough with his eyes focused on my neck I

181

sprung uplifting my feet and kicking him in the chest with my spiked boots. He flew backward and Billy stumbled backward behind me from the force. It gave me enough of an advantage to break from his grasp. I spun around and shoved him back into the wall. In the seconds of commotion, all the twos were suddenly surrounding me. The one still held Chase and the others circled me, waiting. Joe stood up and rubbed his chest. His lips peeled back in anger. "You just signed your contract Titan." He yelled at his minions, "Grab her and hold her down."

They all attacked at once. My fists and feet flew against them taking any hit they could. I waved my arms and grabbed daggers from the air with both hands. The crystals rang as they sliced through the thick air. Someone grabbed my ankle and twisted. I yelped and stabbed him in the arm. A hand snaked out and punched me in the gut and I doubled over out of breath. Fingers grasped my shoulder and squeezed. Bones cracked and still I continued to swing and stab in every direction. As long as no teeth broke my skin, I didn't care what they did to me. I got kicked in the kneecap and my leg gave out. I swung wide catching a few shins and knocking some of them to the ground. Someone kicked me in the chin and I saw stars. I admit that I was starting to get my ass kicked. But honestly, six super strength linebackers against me, it just was not fair. Now five, I could handle, but that extra one was tipping the scale. My lip was bleeding and I was certain that I now had several broken bones. I went down on my knees and with a swift motion I lengthened my dagger until it rang like a sword and swung again in a circle. I managed to take out four this time and they fell back with blood spurting from their knees. Two more continued to pummel me and try holding me down.

I saw Joe standing behind them watching. I saw Chase watching helplessly while the guy holding him smiled. It was that smile that caught me. That grotesque warning of what could possibly come. Time slowed and I saw its eyes. I knew instantly that that was no vamp staring back at me. The madness that gleamed excitedly giving me a shudder up my spine was purely demon. A demon was holding Chase. I knew instantly what the disgusting scumbag would consider entertainment. What could happen to Chase if I didn't get us out of here. Memories flooded me. Blood seeped into my thoughts, just like the blood that was seeping into my clothing, while the vamps tried taking me down. I looked over and the demon was watching me while smelling Chase's hair. It smiled and closed its eyes. I snapped. I screamed in outrage and it sounded like the wild cry of a mythical animal. My razor like wings whipped out and sliced into anything within five feet. Blood splurged outward like fountains. My body shook and my vision burned red as I walked toward the demon holding Chase. It actually stepped back in fear. Billy and the others that could still stand continued their attack, but I brushed them off. Broken bones and cuts would not stop me now. If I could have lit fire, I was sure I would have. My anger boiled up and my body burned. I was a dragon on a rampage and nothing was stopping me. My wings stabbed backward catching Billy and another in the chest.

When I got close enough the demon shoved Chase away and stepped toward me. Like lightning, it slammed into me and stabbed me through the stomach with its razor-like claws. I screeched at the painful burn but still I fought him. It tore into my shoulder and laughed when my blood seeped onto its hands. Its eyes turned black and his razor sharp teeth smiled at me. I stabbed him in the chest with my dagger and he screamed in outrage. I beheaded him mid-scream with the longer blade then I stumbled toward the floor.

I heard Chase call out just before Joe grabbed me from behind. My wings were pressed up against me and useless against him. His mouth reached toward my neck and my head swam with dizzy confusion. I felt the floor against my hands as my strength started to desert me. I started mentally preparing myself for what was about to happen. Joe suddenly let go. There was a small commotion behind me, but I started falling in darkness.

Someone grabbed me from the front. Strong warm arms wrapped around my waist. My wings softened. "Your wings, Angel. Use your wings!"

My head swam and I opened my eyes to Chase looking at me and holding me against him. "Use your wings now!" He screamed at me with desperation. "Fly! Now!"

My mind told my wings to go, and they shot us straight up and through the wooden ceiling. It might have hurt, I wasn't sure. Moonlight blared against my tired eyes. I could not keep them open. My body was numb, bloody and broken in more places than I could count. Chase hung onto me desperately as we catapulted through the sky. I was able to keep my eyes open for a few minutes until I saw his balcony, then they weighed down. "Shit!" I heard him scream at me. "Crimson, stay with me!" His arms banded around me tighter. "Just a little farther!" I pried them open again and managed to at least aim for his balcony before they closed entirely.

Chapter 13

Chase

I wasn't quite sure how we made it to that balcony, but we did. It was no easy landing though. I managed to fall on my ass with only a bruise or two. Crimson on the other hand, had smashed unconscious into my concrete balcony, completely pulverizing at least five foot of railing. After the smoke and debris cleared enough for me to see, I was able to find her laying over the edge completely broken and lifeless. I pulled her up into my arms and held her for a moment. She didn't move, was barely breathing. She was covered in blood from her dark hair to her boots. I was certain nearly all of it was her own. I laid her against me and stroked her wings. After the long nights of sleeping beside her, I had learned how to almost tame her wings while she slept. With a few convincing strokes I could have them softly tucking away. It took only a minute before they shook off the debris and meshed into her skin. I picked her up and carried her inside.

I took her into the bathroom and turned on the shower. Then I carried her inside and held her against me while the water ran red. I quickly stripped her and efficiently cleaned her off. She didn't wake up or even rustle from unconsciousness. I held her against me like a rag doll. When most of the blood was off her skin I shut off the water and carried her back out. I wrapped her up in a towel and carried her to my bed. Grabbing my first aid kit, I immediately went to work. Her body was already healing on the inside, slowly piecing itself back together. The hole in her shoulder and stomach had started to mend leaving a raw and bloody mess. I cleaned, bandaged and taped what I could to help the process. She had bruises, scratches and cuts all over her body. Broken bones in her shoulder, and leg as well as a busted lip and bruised jaw. I cringed when I touched something that I knew hurt. But she didn't move. When I had done all I could do, I gently lay beside her and softly wrapped my arms around her so I would feel her when she woke.

But she didn't. The bright early afternoon sun woke me and she still lay in a deep sleep beside me. I studied her closely. Her skin had lost all color and her breathing was still quiet and choppy. I worried over her and checked all of her injuries before I got out of the bed. Everything had mended a bit, but nothing was healing completely. I sighed at the still angry red flesh of her wounds. I rewrapped everything and tucked the blankets around her. She probably just needed more time, and more rest. I got up and showered then checked on her. No change. I went out and made some lunch hoping the smell of food would wake her, but it didn't. I made myself busy around the apartment doing things that needed done and checking on her frequently. She remained the same all day long. I started to get a strange feeling in my gut that night. She looked no better now than she had this morning and I know that her body usually would have sprung back by now. I moved her onto her side settling pillows in front of her and laying behind her. I slowly stroked her wings against her skin and although her skin trembled, they did not slowly stretch out. I lay beside her for hours, slowly stroking her skin and waiting for a response.

Three days pass much as the first. Me keeping busy, and her asleep in my bed. I needed to go out and get some things. Food for one thing. I knew for a fact that when she woke she was going to be starving. I was tempted to take my new bike knowing that it would get me back faster, but I kind of wanted to ride it with her the first time. Instead, I scribbled a note in case she woke while I was gone and took my car. It slid a little around the bends in the light snow, but nothing I couldn't handle. It was while I was in the first aisle of the store looking at cereals that I felt a burn in my shoulder. A slow tingle like someone was watching me. I glanced over my shoulder and saw two large guys standing in the entrance watching me. I turned back around and slowly glanced at the shelves. I had no doubt that they were looking for me and looking for Crimson. I also knew that they would follow me until they found her. I slowly rounded the corner and stepped into the next aisle. I could hear them shuffling down the first aisle towards me. I had only a split second to decide what to do, and I knew I had to run. I left my cart and bolted to the next aisle and ran down it passing startled people. My heart beat frantically in my chest, but I managed to sneak out the door without seeing them again. I ran to my car and jumped in, starting the engine and peeling tire out of the lot. Before I turned the corner at the street light I saw them in my rearview running out of the store looking for me. I floored it the whole way back to my apartment.

I was praying she was awake so she could tell me what we were supposed to do now. I ran down the hall and it wasn't until I was behind the bolted door that I was able to breathe. My apartment was quiet just as I had left it. I ran to my bedroom and found her lying just as she had been. She didn't look any better and I tried to wake her, but she didn't stir. I knew in my gut that we had to get out of here. If they were able to find me at the grocery store, there was a good chance that they could find out where I lived very quickly. I ran around my apartment grabbing the things that were most important to me. My cash stash, important papers, my camera and camera cards with all of my photos. I packed them into a duffle bag and filled the rest with clothes. I put on two layers of clothing and pulled on my leather jacket. I quickly dressed her in my skinny jeans and sweatshirt that she was now accustomed to wearing all the time. I threw a pair of sweatpants over the jeans and carried her out to the couch. I picked up the phone and called down to the front desk.

"Hey, this is Bill from the fifth floor. I'm waiting for some guys to move some furniture for me, could you tell me if there are two large guys waiting downstairs for me?"

"No sir, no one yet. Would you like me to call when they arrive?"

"Yes please."

"Sure thing Sir."

I hung up and started my bike. I knew it was going to be hard with the bike and Crimson as dead weight, but I had little choice. I didn't want to leave the bike here and there was a good chance that they had already tagged my car. I pushed the bike out into the empty hallway and went back for her. I carried her and the duffel out and locked the door behind me. I knew there was a good chance that my apartment was going to be ransacked very soon. I had taken any papers with me that would lead them to family or friend's houses. My iPad was also tucked into the duffel. The only thing they would find would be an empty apartment with little food, two TV's, and a wiped Xbox. I cringed a little at the loss of my TV's and the Xbox, but looking in my arms, I knew what was most important.

I sat her in front of me and wrapped the duffel around us both, tightening the strap and anchoring her to me a little more securely. I wrapped one arm around her and slowly rode into the elevator being as quiet as possible. I started it as we slowly rode down to the main floor and my heart sped. There was no actress down there now to distract everyone so I needed to move fast. I also had to watch for anyone that was waiting for me. The elevator dinged and the doors slowly slid open. I had a thirty-second window and I cranked the gas as soon as the doors opened wide enough for me to get out. I focused on the door and had a seconds view of the two guys standing at the front desk arguing with the clerk, who was trying to make a phone call. Heads turned and people squealed with surprise as my bike sped through the lobby and towards the door. Luckily the automatic door was already open because someone was standing right beside it. I managed to slide right through and out onto the sidewalk. I know the two guys had spotted me by now and were probably already after us. I didn't have time to look back. Once the tires hit pavement I sped dangerously towards the city limits.

The bike handled amazingly well even though it was December. The tires cut through the small layer of snow like they were made for it. I was starting to get cold, and I knew the ride wasn't helping Crimson at all. I had driven out of the city and done a few circles and loops to be sure I wasn't followed. After a good hour of meaningless driving, I finally made my way to her place. I kept my eyes open as we approached as I had watched her do many times before. No signs of any trespassers, no sign of life even. It was when I pulled into the driveway that I realized I had no way in. She didn't carry keys because she used her balcony on the fourth floor, and her bike had the button for the garage. I was debating the best way to scale the wall up to her balcony without getting killed when my eyes landed on a small button beside the brake of my bike. Curious, I pushed it and sat like an idiot staring when her garage door started to lift. She had actually had an opener installed on my bike. She had basically given me a key to the front door, figuratively. A smile broke out on my face and I then realized how cold my lips were which brought me back to what I was doing. I pulled the bike in beside her Wind Runner and cut the engine as the door closed behind me.

I managed to get her into the house and up into the living room. I laid her on the floor and ran to her room. I yanked her blankets from her bed and dragged them in front of the fireplace. I made a soft cushion for her and pulled her now wet clothes from her body until she wore nothing. I laid her on top of the nest of bedding then put another blanket over top of her. I hit the button to start the fireplace and cranked it up high. I shivered. I walked around the house checking windows and doors to be sure they were secure and covered. I watched outside for a few moments for movement and saw none. I went back to the living room that was already warming up and yanked my own wet clothes off. I left my boxers on and crawled into the blankets beside her. I shivered again and wrapped myself around her still body. I listened to the short gasps of air and the slow beat of her heart for several hours before I fell into my own oblivion.

I woke the next day well into the afternoon. And still my body ached and my brain wanted to return to the blissful sleep. I forced myself to get up and get dressed. I went through the entire house again checking every door and window. I checked outside for footprints in the snow and watched for movement, but nothing changed. I ended up spending the first day cleaning up the already spotless house. The second, I explored her garage and cleaned my bike. I greased it, checked the tire pressures, checked the fluids, then waxed and polished it. The third day, I did hers.

The fourth day I carried her into the shower with me and cleaned her off. By the time I had gently scrubbed her body and hair, my fingers were wrinkled. I dressed her in a small nightgown from her room and laid her back down by the fireplace to slowly comb her hair. She looked worse now. I knew it was mainly because the woman that could eat everything in sight hadn't had a bite in over a week. I kind of figured that was one of the reasons that she wasn't healing either. She had no nourishment. I tried several times to shake her awake, but she never even budged. The fifth day, I ran to a market that I had passed down the road. I had been surviving on boxed soup for four days and knew I needed something else. I filled the saddle bags and my duffel with groceries and carted them back to the house. I made sure I wasn't being followed before I turned back down her road. I made myself a ham and cheese sandwich and went to explore the attic. She had told me that there were a few boxes up there that had belonged to the previous homeowners that had been left behind. I went up to see if anything could be made useful to me. I either needed something to do or I needed something other than bare walls to stare at. Either way, if I didn't find something I was going to go mad. I was actually surprised at the things that I did find. At least ten boxes of Christmas decorations for one thing, four of them brimming with ornaments, and about ten boxes of random junk. Clothes, sewing kits, magazines and old toys. I was staring at the Christmas things when I got an idea. She would probably be pissed when she woke up, but it was worth it. I dragged a few of the ornament boxes downstairs and sat them in the living room. I checked on her again and made my way downstairs for a chainsaw or an ax.

It was hours later when I was finished and I had done a damn good job. The room smelled like Christmas and the lights shone brightly against the bare walls. Decorations sparkled and twinkled against each other. It was a gem in the bare and empty room. I had just checked on Crimson and was unhappy that there was still no change. Her skin was sickly pale, her breathing choppy, her heartbeat faint and even her wounds had yet to fully heal. I knew that there was nothing I could do. I could not take her anywhere or call anyone. She was different and no one would have any idea what to do for her. It irritated and frustrated me that I could do nothing. Absolutely nothing.

I needed to make some real food for my dinner or I wasn't going to be any help to her when she woke up. I decided to make myself a salad and some grilled chicken. I smiled thinking of the time she told me she didn't eat veggies. She was a totally complex and amazing person. I knew I was crazy about her, and the day she had told me she loved me had been the happiest of my life. She completed me. I pulled the chicken from the fridge making extra in case she woke up, as I usually did, and went to work while my mind ran.

That night I first saw her across the smoky bar had been the luckiest damn night of my life. I had been in a bad stink before that night, after the accident and downfall with Megan, things had been rough. Life had been boring, dull and uneventful. My friends had tried for months to get me moving again, but it wasn't until I saw those violet eyes across the room that something in me shifted. I remember seeing her and my brain had stopped functioning. When our eyes met, the only thing I thought of was how much I wanted that woman in my life. Seeing her get in a tangle with the bouncer had been a warning for me to take a step back. Then she had walked into that diner and I knew that it was meant to be. My friends had warned me that she radiated trouble but seeing her hurt and trying to stay strong had pulled at me. Luckily for her, I was able to catch her when she fell. Literally.

Now? Now I was living. I actually enjoyed waking up in the morning, smiled when the sun rose, and laughed like I hadn't done so in years. She had turned my world right side up, even though I knew she felt like she had tipped it over. I knew this relationship was dangerous, but for her I was willing to take on the danger. She was my light in the darkness, and I intended to do anything to keep her there, and keep her happy. I glanced over at her still form beside the fire. I needed her, and no matter how much she denied it, I knew that she needed me too. I finished the chicken and set it aside to cool while I pulled out some vegetables for my salad. I started chopping them and a slow bead of panic started to work its way through me. This was the worst I had ever seen her. Anytime I had ever seen her injured, she had bounced back within a few days. It had been over a week and still she looked no better. I didn't know what to do. I didn't have any idea if I needed to get water or even food into her system so that she didn't starve to death. I had not the slightest clue what was happening or how to fix anything. I slammed the knife down in fast chopping motions taking my frustration out on the lettuce. I didn't even notice until there was a red puddle on the chopping board that I had cut into my hand. I hissed as my brain caught up and my hand started to burn. I turned toward the faucet and ran cold water over the cut. As the water ran red, a voice made its way into my brain.

"Do you know what happens when they drink blood? If you take just enough, but not too much that you kill them, you create a bond. A true bond that can withstand anything in the universe. A bond so strong that only death can break it. It would revive you, heal injuries and make you stronger, but most importantly it would create the ultimate connection. If what I suspect about you, Titan, is true, then a little blood would change your entire world."

196

I froze, standing there in her kitchen watching my blood run down the drain. What if he had been right? What if that was all she needed to pull through this? A little blood. Maybe he had been right and she wasn't just part Dark Angel and part Light. Maybe she had some vampire in her too. I stood there weighing my thoughts. If it helped her, well, it helped. She would wake up pissed as all hell, but she would be alive. If it didn't work? Well, she would be the same as now, and be pissed when she did wake up. If she woke up. I wrapped a few paper towels around my hand and finished making my salad. If I was going to do this, I needed to make sure I was ready. I ate two helpings of salad and three pieces of chicken. I would most likely pass out at the loss of blood, but it would help hold off as long as I could. I cleaned up but left the food covered on the stove in case she woke before me, because I knew for certain that she would be hungry. I grabbed bandages from the bathroom and the sharpest knife from the rack. I shucked off most of my clothes and crawled in beside her. I took a deep breath as I studied her. I was about to do the second craziest thing I had ever done in my life.

The first? Falling for her. I smiled. We had each other, and I intended for it to stay that way. I used the knife to run a long cut above the inside of my wrist. Low enough that I would get maximum blood flow but high enough that I didn't kill myself. I propped her head up onto my knee and squeezing my fist I held my arm above her open mouth. My blood dripped slowly for a second then flowed like a spout. Her mouth darkened with my blood but still I continued. It might have turned my stomach if I wasn't desperate to help her. After a few moments, my vision started to blur around the edges. I felt my body sway the tiniest bit and I closed my eyes. One more minute. I counted to sixty trying not to open my eyes too quickly. I grabbed the bandage beside me and started wrapping my arm tightly. Everything went fuzzy. I used my last bit of energy to wipe the small drop from the corner of her mouth and kiss her forehead then I blacked out.

Chapter 14

Crimson

I burned. Everything felt like it was on fire. My body was too hot, and my skin crawled as the flames licked higher. My lips and throat burned like hot whiskey and I pushed away from the heat. When I pushed, someone groaned beside me. I pulled my eyes apart and felt like I was waking up for the first time in a century. A fire burned close by and when I turned my head I found Chase lying against me. My eyes adjusted letting me see that it was my fireplace and my living room. I didn't remember coming here. Actually, I was having trouble remembering anything at all. I shook my head to clear the cloudiness and saw a knife and bandages lying beside us. My brow raised at the blood on the blade. My skin started to sweat. I needed to get out of the blankets and away from the fire. I shoved off the blankets and pushed up onto my knees. My arms and legs were heavier than usual. They were sore and achy, too. I felt strange. It was confusing.

Then a sudden pang of relief radiated into me. I fell back onto my butt. I wasn't even sure how to explain it. I knew with certainty what the feeling was, as if I was feeling it myself, but at the same time, I knew it was not mine. It was like I was holding two separate souls inside me at one time. I reached toward Chase as confusion and panic mingled together in my brain. I needed to know what was happening. When my fingers touched him I felt paper instead of soft skin. I focused on his arm where there was a reddened bandage tightly woven around his wrist and forearm. I opened my mouth to ask him what was wrong and a little drop of spit fell out onto my leg. I looked down to see a bright red drop of blood. My mind put the images together faster than I could comprehend. The fight, then nothing. The blood, the bandages, the knife. I looked at Chase. His skin was pale, and sickly. His breathing light and airy. His brow furrowed in frustration. Oh shit!! I bolted onto my feet backing away from him. Oh shit. He didn't. He wouldn't. Panic took over. I swallowed and tasted the metallic sweet blood all through my mouth. I gagged. I hurriedly moved backward away from him tripping on my own feet and landing on my ass. My breathing was heavy and stressed while my mind ran with anger and frustration.

"Don't be mad." I heard him rasp from the pile of blankets.

I looked up into his tired blue eyes. "What the hell were you thinking?" I screamed at him. My energy suddenly doubled and I stood in a flash without even realizing I had wanted to. I steadied myself glaring at him.

"There was nothing else I could do." He slowly pushed himself up. It looked painful, but I ignored it.

"You could have left me alone to get better on my own." I gasped in outrage. "I would have been fine!" I spun around and started pacing the room with sudden energy.

I heard him stand. "I did that. It wasn't working."

"It wasn't working? So after a day or two you decided to go mad scientist on me?"

"Ten." He whispered so quietly I thought I misheard.

"What?"

"You have been out for ten days." He told me while watching me.

I froze. Ten days? That was the longest I have ever been out. Even in my worst fights I usually recovered in at most three days.

"You weren't getting better. Your body stopped healing and you were getting worse. There was no one for me to call, and I had no idea what was happening. What did you want me to do? Twiddle my thumbs while you lay here dying?" His last words were bitter with frustration.

I suddenly felt a sudden loss burst into me like before. Once again I knew it wasn't mine. I looked at him. His beard was grown in, his eyes beaten down and his shoulders sagged with invisible weight.

"I can feel you," I whispered.

He watched me. "As I can you." He smiled. "You were severely pissed a moment ago, but you're starting to cool your jets now."

I blinked at him. Why was he glowing? "This is a big deal Chase. This is something that you could be stuck with for the rest of your life."

"A chance I was willing to take, for you to be healthy again."

"What if I'm different now? I could be more dangerous to you." I felt my teeth with my fingertips half expecting large fangs to be popped out like a bad Halloween costume.

"You're still the same you that you were a month ago. You just know a little bit more about yourself now."

Shit. Why was he always right? I watched him for a moment. He was actually glowing. I shook my head to clear the fuzziness from my eyes and he smiled. I felt a waft of happiness from him. This was going to take some getting used to. I walked toward him and realized that the glowing was behind him. He saw where my focus was and stepped to the side. I froze. There, in my living room was the most beautiful Christmas tree I had ever seen in my life. I could smell the fresh pine as I slowly walked toward it. I felt his eyes watching me, waiting. The pine needles were a glistening green and the lights a warm gold. The entire thing was covered from top to bottom in a red garland and all kinds of ornaments. I stood in shock for a moment. I felt a punch of sadness and loss and I fell to my knees.

He was there instantly wrapping his arms around me and hugging my back. "I'm sorry. I didn't know it would hurt you, I will take it down."

I shook my head. "No. Please don't. It's beautiful."

"It hurts you, I can feel your pain."

I turned back toward him. He looked sad as he watched my eyes. "I love it."

He put his hands on my face. "Truly?"

I nodded and smiled. I leaned towards him and gently kissed him. "Thank you," I whispered against his lips. His lips pulled up in a smile and he pulled me back into him.

After a moment of sweet kisses, my stomach growled. Uh oh. His smile widened. "Chicken on the counter." My stomach grumbled in response and he laughed.

Chapter 15

December started to blow by like a blizzard. I started to get used to feeling Chase all the time and he absolutely loved being so in tune to me. We felt what the other was feeling emotionally, if I was sad or angry he knew. If he was excited about something or about to laugh out loud, I knew. It made things interesting as well. The one day I was sitting on his bike while he was talking and he turned toward me and stopped. I felt a tidal wave of passion as his eyes burned and let's just say things got toasty warm in my garage after that.

The second thing that was different now, was that we always knew where the other was. If I woke up and he wasn't beside me I didn't even have to listen to know where he was. I felt him in the kitchen or in the shower, and even one time I knew that he had walked to the market down at the end of the road. It was strange, but it was comforting. The last thing that had changed was that I was different now. For some reason, the blood he had given me, changed me. I was stronger, I was more energetic, and all of my instincts sharpened. I could see, hear and smell more accurately. Did I crave blood? Actually, no. The idea of sucking it down still turned my stomach even though I knew it had saved my life. I never actually felt the sudden need to stick my teeth into him, and for that I was very grateful.

He had explained to me what happened at the store to him and his sudden and dangerous escape. I was angry that they had tracked him down and angry that I had not been able to help, but glad that he had kept his head on straight to get us to safety. He was right, though. They had likely tagged his car and ransacked his apartment looking for information. He had been smart in moving us and quickly. Unfortunately, that meant that they were still looking, and now he had gone into hiding to protect me. I made him write down all the numbers in his cell phone, text all of his friends that he was going out of town on a spur of the moment vacation, and destroy it. We went out and got a prepaid, no-contract phone, just in case.

When we weren't sneaking around trying to be careful, we were having fun. He tried to get me to go ice skating, but I absolutely refused. Instead, we went snowboarding, skiing, and even ice fishing. The last event only lasted about an hour before I chickened out from the cold. We returned to the hilltop down south at least three more times. Each time we sat quietly with each other talking or just staring out into the beyond. We mostly talked about him and his past. We very rarely talked about me, I told him that it still hurt to talk about things and he let me be. He never got angry or frustrated about it, just nodded his head and told me we had time.

It was after the third visit that way that he presented me with a small Christmas gift while we were sitting by the fire in my house.

I stared at it. "I don't have anything for you."

"Doesn't matter, besides it isn't much, just a little thing."

I gingerly took it and unwrapped the red box with a silly green bow. I raised a brow, "When did you manage to sneak this in?" We had after all spent nearly every woken moment together for weeks.

He just winked at me and waited. I opened the box and inside nestled in white tissue paper was a golden ball ornament. It sparkled with gold glitter and written across the face was black, bold lettering which read, "Our First Christmas Together." I looked up at him and smiled.

"It's beautiful."

"Just like you."

My smile broadened. I felt a wave of satisfaction from him and leaned over to kiss him gently. I stood up and walked to the tree. There was a bare branch near the bottom in the front that was begging for attention, so I gently hung the bulb there. I stepped back and studied it.

I felt his eyes on me and I turned my head. His burned brilliantly as he watched. My mouth twitched up in one corner and I bit my lip. It was a marker on the trail we were making, a large marker on a very rocky trail. He smiled at me as he felt what I was feeling. I heard him whisper across to me, "to many more to come."

I sighed and went back into his arms to stare at the tree with him.

We lived like this all through December. Him, laughing when I bellowed out Christmas carols in the shower, smiling at my whistling while he made dinner and trying to be patient when he was teaching me to cook. Me, smiling when I heard him laugh, giggling when I heard him start to sing in the shower and sleeping like a baby in his arms every night.

It was a few short days before Christmas when things went wrong. Chase had convinced me to let him go and see his uncle for Christmas. He had somehow managed to remove my common sense and sucker me into letting him go. It was almost Christmas, after all, and he was sure everyone was worried since he had been out of reach for most of the month. It was way too dangerous to take the bikes, so I told him we would fly. It's not easy to fly in the cold and snow. It actually sucks. For one thing, it's cold. For another, it's hard to flap your wings if they are freezing over with ice. But, it was better than the bus, so we flew. When we got to his uncle's, I dropped him off and scouted the perimeter of the building. I needed to be careful in order to keep him safe. There wasn't anyone hanging around, no one suspiciously waiting at the corner, or anything standing out to my trained eye. After about half an hour, I went to the door and let myself in. I shucked off my leather jacket and shivered for a few minutes standing in the doorway trying to let my wings dry out a little before I tucked them away. They were still dripping wet when footsteps suddenly rounded the corner and Mandy almost ran into me.

"Oh! There you are." Her eyes widened as she studied my wings. "I was just coming to find you."

I shivered again. "Sorry, just trying to dry a bit."

"Is that why you're hiding here?" She shook her head and grabbed my hand pulling me towards the living room. It was brimming with the same faces from Thanksgiving and they all stared at me in shock. I knew they all had known what I was, I had just been trying to keep it on the down low. Mandy just dragged me in and gently shoved a few people out from in front of the fireplace and pushed me into their place. My face heated from the warm flames.

"Better?"

I smiled and turned and sat right in front of it and spread my wings out so they could dry. "Yes." I smiled up at her. "Thank you."

She plopped right down in front of me. "Good. Now I don't want you to freak out but..."

Before she could finish, the people in the room suddenly overcoming their awe surrounded me with greetings. I was given hugs and a few even asked permission to touch. I shook my head at them and after a few minutes they gave me some room. My wings started to feel lighter. I gave them a shake and they stretched out before gently collapsing into my back. I stayed where I sat, letting the rest of my body warm up. I had managed to wear jeans and a green shirt, yes green, I do own one, that covered from my hips to my wrists, with the exception of my shoulder blades and spine. I shrugged, give a little, take a little. My hair, on the other hand, was a wet mess of rings and curls. It also started to dry and I tried to tame it with my fingers while I sat waiting for Mandy to continue. After a few minutes, she did frantically.

"As I was saying, I don't want you to freak out but they just got here. No one had any idea they were coming in, I suppose it freaked them out when they couldn't get hold of Chase and no one else had heard from him in a few weeks, so they just kind of showed up unexpectedly..."

"Who?" I asked trying to calm her down. She took a deep breath and opened her mouth to answer me.

"And just where exactly is this girl that thinks it is perfectly alright to take you away on vacation without letting anyone know where you're going?" A woman walked in brimming with a pissed off attitude and waving her arms around demanding answers as she walked. She had a business cut dress suit in bright red on and gold jewelry all over her wrists, neck and dangling from her ears. She had jet black long hair pulled back into a tight ponytail and electric blue eyes that sparked cold flame. The man that walked in behind her was tall and muscular, but not overly done. He had a sharp superstar face with tan skin, green eyes and a soft generous smile. When he spotted me, his face lit up and a smile stretched across his perfectly white teeth, just like someone else I knew. Oh shit.

Mandy whispered beside me, "His parents."

Chase came in the room behind them followed by my biggest fan, Uncle Josh. When Chase's eyes found mine, he smiled and shrugged. When everyone's eyes managed to land on me, Mandy gave me a gentle nudge. I slowly stood up grinning at the picture I probably made. Twenty-something, dark wild hair, out of this world purple eyes, wet jeans, scant shirt, and defiant non-human attitude. I sighed, story of my life.

I slowly walked toward them and Chase met me in the middle. He grabbed my hand and gently tugged me toward his parents. "Mom and Dad, this is Angel. Angel, my mom, Susan, and my dad, William."

I smiled at them. His dad came forward and took my hand firmly in his. "Nice to meet you my dear, anyone that can take out Josh here in one swoop is good in my book." I grinned as he put an arm around Uncle

Josh and patted him on the belly. He grumbled in reply.

His mother studied me. "Yes, obviously violent, and defiant. Not really sure those are good qualities," she glared at her husband. "Chase tells me that you surprised him with a three-week vacation to the mountains. I really must question your upbringing if you think that people can just disappear without telling anyone else where they are going and how long they will be. It worried us sick."

"Mother, I told you that my phone was giving me issues. It was not her choice for me to lose contact with everyone." Chase answered.

She scowled, then looked at me, waiting.

I smiled and shrugged. "I apologize, Susan. I'm afraid I do not have any family to worry over me, so I simply did not think of Chase's situation as one to cause a fuss over." I bit my lip, this was hard making up shit to not piss people off. "I'm terribly sorry that you were worried and I will know to be more diligent in the future."

She watched me for a moment then nodded once. "Good." She was about to turn away when she paused and turned back to me. "No family?"

"No."

"At all?"

"None."

"Why? Were you an orphan?"

"No, my family was taken from me. Violently," I added to cease the questioning, but she continued.

"When?"

I had to tread carefully. I didn't know if she knew about my 'dead girl issues' or not. If I told her ten years ago, she might question why if I was so young wasn't I put into foster care, then things would just get complicated. "When I was nineteen."

She seemed to want to know every detail, trying to trip me up somewhere so she pushed. "Accidental?"

I was tired of the game and my irritation grew. "I do not consider the slaughter of a father, mother and three brothers accidental, do you?"

The room was silent. No one moved, and I thought perhaps they even held their breath.

"Hmmm, and yet, here you are." She whispered so only I could hear her.

My eyes flashed. I felt Chase's tension, sadness, and fear.

I stepped closer so that we stood nose to nose and I whispered to her.

"The very same notion that crosses my mind every second of every day through eternity."

Her eyes widened, and she took a step back, breaking eye contact.

"So, is it time to eat yet? We have a long flight back tonight and I need my sleep."

Everyone sucked in air as if the room was suddenly safe again. Mandy headed towards the kitchen, Chase hugged me and held me for a moment while his parents walked off to visit with someone. His uncle watched me from over Chase's shoulder. He didn't say anything, just watched.

It wasn't easy, this family thing. Luckily Chase and Mandy had dinner ready within ten minutes and we were able to eat with happy chatter between us all. Well, his Dad at least chatted happily with me. His Mother quietly watched me under her lashes while his uncle blatantly stared at me with disapproval. No one else had any kinds of issues with me, it was just those two. I shrugged them off. I had other things to deal with.

"They love me," he whispered in my ear when we stepped outside. "In their own special way." I scoffed against the cold wind. He watched my eyes. "I'm sorry she was so hard on you. She isn't really the loving and warm type."

I raised a brow at him. "Really? I hadn't noticed."

He smiled at me and kissed me quickly. "Are we homebound?"

I shivered in the cold. "Yes. Home, shower, fire, and food."

"That's it?"

"What did you have in mind?"

He shrugged. "I don't know, a movie, coffee, laser tag, bowling..."

I raised a brow. "Bowling?" I dragged out the word trying to emphasize the point that he had just asked me if I wanted to go bowling.

He laughed. "Come on then. We can start walking and see where our feet lead us."

I shivered again and leaned into him for warmth. He threw an arm around me as we started walking down the city street. We passed a few people. The ones that were crazy enough to brave the cold. My nose turned red and started to lose feeling, but Chase just kept walking. My back started to itch, and I kept looking over my shoulder. Something felt off.

"I know a good theater two streets over," he squeezed me into him. "I used to go there with my uncle all the time growing up. It's just a little farther."

I tried to keep my teeth from chattering, but by the next street they started to shake. I still felt that strange feeling. The muscles at the back of my neck tensed a bit. We were passing by a dark alley when my alarms went up. Chase froze beside me feeling my sudden tension. My eyes searched the darkness and found three shadows waiting. I pushed Chase behind me and we backed away. Then laughter sounded to our left and hisses came from our right. We froze in the middle of the street surrounded. To our left, demons, two of them. Blackened eyes and sharp teeth. They smiled at us and I recognized the one. He was the demon that we had run into that night after the diner. Apparently, he had recovered. To our right, vampires. Five of them. Level twos and threes by the looks of them. All red-eyed and looking thirsty.

Out of the darkness came a new face. A woman, in a white pinstripe business suit with blonde hair, pulled back into a tight bun and red lipstick staining her lips. She wore sunglasses even in the darkness. She radiated power, and when she walked toward us, her feet barely touched the ground. She glided. Witch. My hackles went up. She was shadowed on each side by large human males. They were probably her consorts, or they wished they were. They all slowly walked closer, forming a tight wall around us. I felt Chase's fear like a punch to the gut. My hands fisted. Chase turned and put his fists up and his back against mine. I watched the witch. She seemed like she was the one in charge of this little mission.

"Titanium Angel." Her voice crackled like fire. She studied me then her eyes went to Chase. "And Chase." I barred my teeth at her and felt Chase's surprise. She clucked her tongue. "Marco told me that you had delicious taste, Titan, I think I have to agree." The vampires licked their lips like hungry dogs. She watched them with mild interest. The cold whistled around us as my heart sped against my chest. She smiled. "I have a little experiment to try and luckily, I have chosen you two to be my lab rats. Aren't you thrilled?" She smiled coldly. Her eyes landed on Chase again. "And I do hope it works, I have uses for you, Chase."

I snatched daggers from the air and threw them at the vamps. They flew fast and froze dropping to the ground a few feet from their targets. They hissed at me and smiled. She slowly shook her head at me. "Oh please cooperate, Titan, things will go so much easier that way."

"Go to hell."

She laughed. "Been there darling, done that."

She waved her arms and the air cooled. Snow started to whip around us making my body shudder. It became a tornado of snow and ice jabbing against my skin and hazing my vision. Chase leaned against me and grabbed my hand squeezing hard. I could no longer see anything, and my body started to freeze. First, I lost feeling in my fingers, then in a matter of seconds, I had no feeling at all. I felt the fast beating of Chase's heart right behind me, then, I felt nothing.

Chapter 16

I shivered in my sleep. It was strange, waking up and not feeling the warmth of Chase or the softness of my bed. I felt Chase, felt him right beside me in my mind, but he felt strange. I tried to move my body to shake off the cold, but I couldn't lift my arms or legs. I pried open my eyes and shivered once more in darkness. No light, no warmth, no softness. My eyes widened as I remembered what happened. My body shook, something was wrong with Chase. I searched in the darkness for him, knowing that he was close. When I jerked my body, chains rattled and water splashed. I was laying in freezing cold water, chained to a concrete slab in a cold room. The water was up to my ears and sound came in and out as the water level moved. I heard him, breathing heavy but breathing. "Chase?" My voice cracked.

The water sloshed and more chains rattled. "Crimson?"

"Chase, are you hurt?"

"No. Just tied up at the moment. You?"

"I'm ok."

He sighed heavily. "How do we get out of this one?"

I pulled at the chains holding me down. They were not budging. "Not sure."

"I'm sorry, we should have just gone home like you said. We would have never gotten in this mess if I had listened to you."

"It's not your fault Chase. Let's just get out of it."

"Yeah." I heard him strain and chains rattle once more.

"Where the hell are we?"

"Don't know. I know it's fucking cold and wet."

"Right. Got that."

He sighed. "What is that bitch going to do to us?"

I cringed. I had no idea. But hopefully, she had liked Chase enough to let him live. I opened my mouth to tell him to be strong and patient and we would be fine, but a door opened with a loud creak. Artificial light streaked in blinding me for ten seconds. When my eyes refocused, I scanned the room. We were in some sort of underground cellar by the look and feel of things. Cement blocks lined the walls, and sludge and grime covered the waterlogged floors. I was in the center of the room on a slab with about three inches of water surrounding me. I tilted my head back and found Chase on his knees a few feet from my head. His arms were pulled back around a steel column, and his ankles were shackled together. His shoulders sagged and his head was tilted down trying to avoid the sudden light. There was a smear of blood on his shirt so he likely had a broken nose or a split lip.

My gaze flew back to the door where the demon I recognized was shuffling through the door dragging a large water hose with him. The woman from before followed him in, along with her minions. Her black boots should have clicked on the cold floor, but they barely whispered as she walked. She still wore her sunglasses and her pinstripe suit. She glanced around the room and her lips twitched. She turned back to us and smiled at Chase.

"I'm just ever so curious how the two of you managed to find each other."

She leaned over me so that she stood just above me. Her red lips stretched across white glamorous teeth. "I can certainly see what you're attracted to, Titan," her eyes lifted to Chase again, "But you, Chase." She clucked her tongue. "Just what exactly do you see in this...monster?"

He strained against his shackles and snarled pulling open his split lip. "Don't talk about her like that."

She laughed, a light and musical sound. "No? What exactly do you think you have stumbled upon here? An angel?" She laughed again. "Is that what she has led you to believe? That she is a perfect little angel?

That you two can live happily ever after for the rest of your lives." She giggled. "How adorable. How pathetic." She glided over to Chase and pulled his head up by the chin. "My little Chase, how you have grown. Not to worry, soon enough the Titan will be a memory and you can serve me."

He jerked his chin away from her grip. "Over my dead body."

She laughed. "Momentarily, my dear, momentarily."

My heart leaped into my throat. So she planned to kill me and turn him. She was going to kill him. My body froze with fear and my heart slowed. She glided back towards the door and nodded at the demon. He twisted off the end of the water hose and dropped it to the ground. Water gushed out onto the ground by my feet. I instantly felt the ice cold water splashing against my legs. I shivered as it surrounded me and slowly rose against my cheeks. The cold water was paralyzing. It froze my body from the outside in, slowly creeping along my skin and into my bones. I had to lift my head slightly so that I could still see and somewhat hear. She nodded once more to the demon and he sloshed toward me and shoved against the slab that held me. He strained and pushed with all his strength until the slab slid along the floor toward Chase. The demon pushed me until I was right beneath Chase's face. His blue eyes were wide with worry and strained with fear. I shook my head at him and tried to push calmness and strength into him. His lips were turning blue in the cold and I felt his body tremble with cold and fear. He watched me, and then his eyes jumped up to the demon and heart-stopping fear punched me in the gut as his eyes widened and he started to freak out. He pulled at his chains above me as the freezing cold water climbed along my cheeks. He yanked and jerked his body trying to break free. I saw his mouth moving and felt the water tremble as he screamed in rage. I pushed my frozen muscles and tilted my head towards the reason for his distress. I had just a seconds view of a dagger before it slammed into my body. Fire burned in my chest and pain screamed its way along my senses. Cold and heat mingled together swirling in my head and dizziness swamped me. My vision blurred and I sucked in air.

The woman waited until the demon pulled my head up far enough so that I could hear. "Now, Titan, I have waited nearly a decade to cause you problems, so please do not interrupt. I have killed your kind before, almost have it down to a science. I'm going to kill you, and you will die slowly. So slowly, that your loverboy here will watch your blood slowly drain from your body." I struggled to train my eyes on her. She smiled at me. "He can watch it drip from your body, drop by drop until there is not an ounce left. Then he can watch you take the very last breath through your crackled lips and just before you completely leave this earth, you can watch him become mine." The demon dropped my head back into the water. I could hear my heart pumping against the water and I tilted my head back up to Chase. He watched me. Our eyes held as he struggled against the chains. I felt the dread slowly roll over my heart. I didn't know if it was mine, his or both. He tucked his body down closer to me and rubbed his face against mine while we both trembled. His lips traveled through the water to my ear and the words "I love you" rumbled against my skin. My eyes widened as he lifted his head and kissed me. It should have been a moment of pure connection where it was just us in the entire world and nothing could come between us, but he was yanked away seconds after his lips touched mine. Water splashed into my eyes and I shook my head trying to clear them.

More water splashed into my face and I strained to see above me. The demon had pulled Chase back up and shoved him back against the column. He moved behind, holding him up while a vamp splashed over to them. I watched helplessly as it sunk its teeth into Chase's neck. I tried to pull up and reach him, but my body was useless. The water was freezing along my limbs turning into ice. My fingers crackled as I moved them. My hair was frozen in the water and I had to yank my head to lift it and see what was happening. Through the blurriness, I found the woman standing at the edge of the water with a hand outstretched and white wind flowing from her hand and freezing the water that held me in its grasp. Chase screamed out above me as his adrenaline deserted him and the pain of the bite finally hit him. The vamp pulled back, blood dripping from his lips and fangs. Chase slumped forward, sucking air into his lungs as his blood dripped down his neck and onto his chest. My head was too heavy to lift and my body was frozen solid to the concrete beneath me. Even the blood that ran from my burning chest was no longer warm, it was cold and slow.

Water sloshed in my ears as I tried to move my head from side to side.

"Chase," I called out to him. My voice broke. I couldn't hear myself, but I felt the sudden break as even my voice started to fail me. He opened his eyes and we watched each other. I spoke to him even though I wasn't even certain he could hear me. "It's ok. We will be ok." His eyes frantically watched me as a slow burn started running through his blood. His body turned to tremors. "Chase. It's ok. We can get through this." His eyes found mine again and his lips peeled back in pain.

I heard her voice again, but I couldn't hear her words. Chase broke eye contact with me and looked up. My eyes tried to follow, but I could not see her. The demon splashed through the icy water back towards me. Chase fought the chains and shackles again. He snarled and screamed in rage above me. The demon pulled the knife from my chest and positioned it against my neck. I wouldn't feel it. My body was almost completely numb and unresponsive. My pain was in my heart. I wasn't stone hearted. I had a lot to lose. Chase was going to watch me bleed out and then I didn't know what would happen to him. He was everything to me and I knew that this would kill him, this would break him. I wanted to tell him that I loved him, but I already felt myself draining. I was going to die, again. And this time, I doubted I was coming back. He fought and jerked against his restraints like a wild animal all while his eyes stayed on mine. Suddenly, the water glowed blue. It sparked and crackled with bright blue neon lights and those lights raced through the water and into Chase. He screamed as his body froze with tension. I screamed as his pain punched into me. I screamed his name. He twisted and snarled as blue electricity wrapped around his body.

It was her. I knew it was her. Using her witchcraft to electrocute him through the water. I screamed his name until my throat burned. When it stopped he slumped down toward me. His body jerked and trembled as little blue aftershocks zapped him. When his eyes opened, they were full of pain, fear, and hate. I felt the knife push into the side of my neck and knew that this was it. This was my fate. I was a Forgotten, and a Forgotten has no hope. I may have cheated my fate for ten years, but now, now that I had finally found someone to find me, find the real me, fate had caught up. And it was going to break us both. I looked up into his swirling blue eyes and I smiled. "See you around, Rockstar." He broke. I felt his heart break and it broke mine. His eyes squeezed shut with the pain and tears fell down his cheeks. When he opened them I felt the knife move across my throat. We kept our eyes on each other. I was grateful we at least had this moment. This moment where our eyes touched and through our eyes our souls would connect and hopefully stay together for eternity. He screamed again as I felt a thick wetness race down my neck. Then blue sparks flared up around us once more. Our moment was once again stolen from us. I tried to tell him, tried to calm him with my words of love, but I choked on my blood as ice crawled up my lips. The blood didn't drip ever so slowly, giving us the time that we needed. It ran, and with it ran Crimson. I lost myself into the icy water. I lost myself not even knowing that I had been there in the first place. Chase had found me, and as he screamed in pain and torment, I finally found myself, there bleeding away into nothingness. Coldness took all the feeling from my body and I felt nothing. I looked up as darkness surrounded me and the last thing I saw was Chase, the love of my life being murdered while I lay there unable to save him. In my mind I called out to him, I had to let him know. That he had saved me. That he had found me. I love you, Chase. Darkness closed in and I felt nothing.

Chapter 17

I can't explain death to you. I have been through it twice, and still have no words to describe it to you. I would like to tell you that it is like falling asleep, that you just drift off on a sleepy cloud and into nothingness. No pain, no regrets, and no heartbreak. Perhaps for the lucky ones, that is what happens. For the rest of us, we are not so lucky. It is like falling into a black hole and not knowing what is real and what your mind has created. You can still hear things. It's almost like you're standing over your dead body, but you can't see anything. You hear, and you feel in your heart, but nothing else. It's like falling asleep and waking in a panic because you slept too long. Only you're not awake, you're dead. You died and all the pain that you carry in your heart and soul surrounds your mind. It reaches out and wraps its cold and numb fingers around you cutting off all feeling except the pain. You always feel the pain. I fell into the blackness that night. I fell and fell and fell, and yet again, there was no one there to catch me. I heard Chase crying out in pain and heartbreak. I heard him for what seemed like hours as my body cooled in front of him and they left him alone to die. They let him die. I hoped with every ounce of hope that I could muster, that his death was quick, and although I wanted him to survive and move on, part of me hoped that he had not. Part of me hoped that he had gotten that death that I mentioned before. The death of the lucky ones. I hoped that he was drifting on a sleep cloud into bright lights and happiness. For hours, I fell and floated and listened to him scream and cry and suffer. As I fell, he got farther and farther away. Our connection was being severed. Death was claiming us.

When I felt my body again, I was wishing that I had not. First, I felt the cold. It lay upon me like the thick fog of an eerie night. Then, I felt the giant hole in my heart. It was an empty space of nothingness. A blank feeling that expanded like a balloon of needles and knives. It took my breath away. The pain that radiated from the wounds on my body were dull aches to my numb limbs. I felt like I was missing everything inside of me. That I was not altogether, not all there. When I pried my eyes open, I had to blink a few times to try to understand my surroundings. I was in the same room, laying on the same slab. I jerked my chin up to find Chase, and he was gone. My eyes flew around the room, but I was completely alone.

Nothing moved, and the air was stale. I had been alone for a long time. The water that surrounded me was cold, but the ice was gone. When I lifted my arms, the chains fell away. I struggled to sit up and felt my neck. The cut across my throat was a raised scar, and the stab in my chest a mere scratch. I had to have been out for a few days at least. I studied the chains around my ankles and found them melted. When I moved my legs, they slid off and into the water. I slowly stood on shaky legs and studied the room. Where was Chase? He had died, I had felt him die. But why was he not left here to rot like I was? Upon closer study, I found the steel column twisted and marred and broken. It was snapped in half with deep cuts gutted into the sides. The chains and shackles were nothing but bits and pieces in the shallow water. Black burn marks streaked the walls and ceiling. And blood, blood lay on every surface. It lay in a diluted pool on the slab beneath me, it splattered against the walls, and it lay in the gray stagnant water. It was not all mine. My throat closed up and pain seared my chest and head. Chase. I stepped through the still water causing ripples to flow outward. I walked to the door that had been left wide open and barely hung from one hinge and listened. Nothing. I stalked out into a hallway that was marred with deep grooves in the cement walls, and upstairs that were littered with blood stains.

Death littered the stagnant air. I found the first body at the top of the stairs. It was lying across the doorway. A vamp with its throat torn out. The second was along the wall in the next hallway. It had been a demon, now nothing more than a headless corpse. I slowly moved past it and into a living space. Whoever had been here, had left in a hurry. Food and drinks sat untouched, belongings abandoned and the dead left to rot. More bodies behind the couches, and another in the doorway leading to more stairs. Sunlight streaked down from these stairs, so I stepped over the body of one of the witch's humans and crept up the stairway. At the top, bright sunlight filtered in on cold winter air through the open doorway. Noises could be heard in the distance, but nothing to lead me in the direction that I wanted to go in. The direction to find Chase, the direction to hope that he was alive, the direction to hope that he wasn't. The house was abandoned and had been for a few days judging by the smell that was starting to circulate throughout it.

I did the world a favor and turned all of the dials on the stove on, as well as the oven, and lit a match. I grabbed some gasoline from the neighbor's garage and spread it through the house to take care of the rest.

Chase, and whoever was chasing him, was long gone. So when I lifted my tired and confused red wings and soared into the cold winter day the explosion shook the earth behind me. I began my search, knowing that it was more than hopeless. Chase had died, that much I was sure of. But something else had risen in that basement. Something angry, powerful and out for blood. Chase might be a vampire now, or even a warlock. My final thought made me cringe. There was even the slightest possibility that he had become a Lost One. A Forgotten. The woman had said that she wanted to use us for an experiment, maybe she was trying to create a Forgotten. Maybe, she had succeeded. For some reason, and I wasn't at all sure why, she had failed to kill me. She had assumed I was dead and left me to rot. Her mistake. Now I was going to search every corner of the earth to find her until she led me to Chase.

First thing I did, was fly home. In my heart, I hoped that he would be there, quietly waiting for me. But in my mind, it was a far away dream. My house was empty, quiet and lonely. I showered and changed quickly knowing that time was of the essence. I had a ten-second view of the new scar I was brandishing on my neck and zipped up my jacket. I glanced at the clock to find that it was December 22nd. I had only been out for two days, which was surprising. I would have thought my body would need more time to bounce back. I was out the door again within twenty minutes and I headed for his apartment. It had been ransacked, judging by the dust at least a month beforehand. No one had been there since. I flew to his uncle's, and quietly snuck inside. His uncle was asleep in his bed and no one else was around. I zipped to the diner that I knew Marco made a point to visit on a daily basis and walked in. I spotted him at the bar before he saw me. I walked up behind him and wrapped my arm around his neck and squeezed. People around us froze and I yanked him back off the stool. "Outside," I snarled and pulled him out with me. He did not struggle, he knew what I would do to him. I pulled him around to the back of the building and shoved him up against the wall.

He choked. "Red, I would say I was pleased to see you, but you seem a bit pissy this morning. I heard you have been stirring up more trouble than usual lately."

I smacked his head off the bricks and snarled at him. "Marco, I want information, and I want it now."

He smiled at me. "Information is what I got baby, just say the word and for the right price my knowledge is yours."

I smiled back at him and put a razor-edged wing against his throat. "How about if the price is your life."

The smile fell from his face. "Whatever you need."

"Good. Now, the witch bitch that you sold me and my human out to, what do you know about her?"

Sweat beaded on his brow. "I would never sell you out, Red..."

I pushed the blade in and he sucked in air as a drop of blood fell. "She goes by Tundra. I don't know much about her, just that she is some kind of witch. Rumor has it that she used to be more, but somehow lost some of her powers." I waited. He did not continue.

"That's all?"

He shrugged. "It's not like we sit down for tea and biscuits every week."

I snarled at him. "If you hear from her again, I want to be the first to know..."

His eyes flashed and I shoved him harder. "You already did."

He cringed. "Yesterday. She sounded pissed. Told me that if I heard any news about your human that I was to let her know right away." He watched me closely. "Told me that he was now a monster and highly dangerous. That I was to treat the situation with utmost care. Call her immediately and track him." My fingers numbed.

"And?"

"Might have mentioned that you had been eliminated and he would likely be seeking revenge." He tried to smile again. "And here you are."

It was my turn to smile. "Maybe you need to learn a lesson, Marco." His eyes widened as I put more pressure against his neck. "I am a Forgotten. I am The Forgotten. I have more power in my hands that you hold in your entire body." I might have exaggerated, but I needed to get my point across. "I can kill you in my sleep without lifting a finger. No matter who comes after me, no matter what they do to me, no one can kill me." I reached down to unzip my jacket and his eyes flew to my throat. "Your witch friend sliced my throat and staked me. She let all of the blood drain from my body, and here I am. Alive and kicking. Can you do the same?" I pushed harder. "Shall we find out?"

He panicked. "No. No, of course not."

"You sold information on me, Marco. This was not a good idea. I could even say that you are the core reason for my very irritating dilemma right now."

He shook his head in denial. "Never again. I shall never again betray you."

"So," I whispered, "when you hear, see, or even smell something. Who are you going to call?"

He sucked in air as blood dripped from his neck His eyes stayed glued to mine. "You, Titan. You."

I dropped him and he fell to his knees. "Good." I straightened. "Anything else I need to know?"

He scrambled for footing on the ground. "If she finds out she will kill me."

I watched him. When he looked up I smiled. "Oh, just call me. I have a little-unfinished business with the bitch."

He nodded suddenly under the false impression that I would protect him, and I laughed coldly. Fool. I didn't give second chances.

I spent two days searching aimlessly. Just traveling everywhere for some kind of hint that he was there. If I found any trace of him, it was a trail of destruction and fear. The vamps feared him, and the demons whispered about him. He was stirring the waters, and although I was glad to know he was alive, he was tipping the balance too much. One thing was clear, Chase had become a Forgotten. From what Marco had told me and the way the undead watched over their shoulders with edgy suspicion, I knew that things were not going well. I wanted to be there for him, to help him through this. He should be in hiding, not tearing the world to shreds. My search turned frantic Christmas Eve day, and I traveled to his special hillside above the ocean in the off chance that he had gone there. I sat on that cliff and waited. It was the first time that I had sat and just let my brain take over. Memories scored my mind of our visits here. Then, I found myself replaying my life since I had met him. My heart hardened and my hope dwindled. I stayed there all afternoon and well into the eve, begging anyone that was listening to help me find him. The emptiness that was my heart and soul expanded until I was numb all over and felt nothing but loneliness. I was falling apart and soon there would be nothing left.

Chapter 18

I laid there on the bland beige carpet of my living room floor. The cold draft that swept through the open window was bitter, but I did not notice it. I had come home moments ago and sank to the floor in front of our tree. I had nothing left. I was numb. I lay there staring up into the shiny reds and golds that colored the tree. The bright white lights that glowed should have been warm, but they weren't. A clock strikes midnight in the far distance and the sound echoed through my brain. It was Christmas, and for the first time in my life, I actually felt lost. There was no connection to Chase racing through my nerves. I felt no fear from him, no confusion, and no love. I couldn't feel if he was close like I used too. I felt nothing. I knew that he was out there somewhere feeling all of those things. He was feeling everything that I had felt ten years ago. Lost, confused and standing on the bridge of insanity. My body felt empty and hollow. I felt like I had failed him, like someone had failed me all those years ago. I should have been there for him, should be with him now. I knew the fate of a Forgotten. For all I knew he could be dying right this second on the other side of the earth, and I would still feel nothing. Absolutely nothing. I reached up to the golden globe that hung suspended by my face. Black letters reading "Our First Christmas Together" across the surface. It shattered in my tightened fist. My eyes blurred. I rolled onto my side and buried my face into my arm putting the bright tree to my back. I trembled and like a dam my wall cracked and tumbled under the pressure. Tears fell from my eyes and I sobbed. My wings curled around me. They trembled with loss and pain but still they comforted me. I sobbed for Chase, I sobbed for my heart, and I grieved for him.

Chapter 19

Chase

I stood outside the open window that was frosted over with the cold hands of winter as a clock chimed midnight in the distance. I had no idea how long I had been standing here watching her. My thoughts and feelings were not my own. It had taken days for my mind to remember where she lived. I watched her lay there looking lost and hopeless and part of me wanted to go to her and comfort her. Hold her against my body and chase away the cold I knew she was feeling. She reached up and shattered the bulb that I had bought for us thinking we would have many holidays together after today. Part of me saddened, but a new part of me laughed. Laughter filled my head and my blackened wings twitched excitedly against me. She turned toward me, but she did not see me. I saw her body twitch when the first sob broke free. My fists tightened as her sobs filtered through the open window and blew into me. Her reddened wings twisted around her trying to comfort her. I watched as the very tips darkened. They trembled and shook against her, and the feathery edges blackened like charcoal. My lips stretched into a grin of satisfaction while my heart broke. My mind twisted in so many directions. I wanted to go to her and end her suffering, and I wanted to stand here and enjoy her pain. My fists squeezed and blue electricity sparked in my palms. It traveled through me with warmth and raw power. The snow beneath my bare feet steamed away and my eyes heated. My stomach growled as my heightened focus landed on her neck. That soft beautiful skin that pumped in time to her heartbeat. I felt my heart match her rhythm as my teeth ached. The sharp edges pulled forward painfully and I wanted to go to her again. Only this time I wanted to pull her to me and sink my fangs into her soft skin. I wanted to taste her, I wanted to drink her essence into me. I cringed and I snickered. I wanted to kill her.

A sneak peak of Zirconium, coming soon!

Crimson

One. Two. I take a deep breath. Three! I let out the clutch and the beast beneath me roars into motion. The world around me becomes a white blur as I speed uncaringly through this winter wonderland. I am cold. I'm always cold now. Almost like my insides are covered in frost and icicles. My lips lose feeling and my limbs tremble, but I push the throttle to go faster. It is February and I could not wait a moment longer to bring my bike out from its slumber in the garage. It had been shut in since November, but my restlessness has taken over. My tires slide across the ice and snow and my ass end tries to come up beside me, but I steer into it and straighten out without care. My beautiful bike was once my prized possession, now I had nothing that I cared about. A face with piercing blue eyes flashed into my memory and I cringe against the hurt. I push the clutch and shift into a higher gear pushing myself into a faster speed. I didn't have the energy to reminisce on the past. I could only move forward. I was currently heading into the city, to a vampire owned bar that would drag up memories that I was not ready for. Marco, my Dark Angel snitch that was working both sides of the system had just called and informed me that the owner, Joe had just had a run-in with Tundra. Tundra was the bitch that had torn me open and left me to die. Literally. Marco told me that there wasn't much being said about the encounter, but it was possibly something to do with my human. I cringed again, blocking out the memories as long as I could.

In a few moments, the building loomed in the distance with neon letters glowing that read The Blue Room. I didn't bother parking on the street, didn't bother parking at all. I lifted my front end up and drove right through the doors. Screams echoed in the darkness and glasses shattered when people dropped their drinks in surprise. I didn't give them the time of day. I was after the boss. I turned my bike toward the steps and roared up them onto the next floor. Vamps hissed from the shadows as they backed away and I continued down the hallway to the familiar room. Once inside I rolled to the center of the room and put it in neutral. I gassed it a few times to make sure everyone knew I was here. I wasn't in the mood for games. Once it quieted again I hit the kill switch and threw down the kick stand. I slowly inspected the room. It looked just the same as it did before. With the exception of the gaping hole in the ceiling that was showing a mediocre patch job. The last time I had been here, they had almost gotten me. Almost gotten us. I shook my head to clear it and heard the movements outside in the hallway as they scampered around unsure what to do. I rose from the black leather seat and sauntered over to the chair that I knew was Joe's and plopped down in it kicking my heels up along the armrest and waited. I knew I wouldn't have to wait long.

I twisted my long dark hair around my fingers and stared impatiently with my violet eyes. I liked to make an entrance.

I had long ago categorized the vamps into three groups, the smart ones that were going to get somewhere with their existence, the ones that could get somewhere, and the ones that had no hope of ever becoming more than a bloodsucking stupid creep. They came first, the threes. They crept in like shadows over a graveyard. They sucked away any light and warmth that the room held and they silently waited in the darkness. I knew they were there, but I gave them no acknowledgment, I wasn't interested in their sick games. They whispered, chuckled, and they licked their lips. I cared not. Next came the twos. They strolled into the room with their nice clothing and large bodies. They gazed at me momentarily and went to the mini bar and fixed their drinks before sitting themselves into their chairs as if preparing for a theatrical show. They, like me, seemed to have little interest in what was happening around them. When I heard the next group coming I smiled at the slight uneven limp that I heard between harsh breaths. Apparently Joe was a little worse for the wear. Why did this make me happy? The last time I had seen him he had left me in bad shape. He paused and composed himself outside in the hallway before stepping through looking all powerful, boss-like. My foot twitched impatiently. I raised a brow to where he stood watching me. His two minions stood behind him statue like and waiting. One of them was Billy and I held back from taunting the idiot. Joe smiled at me. I studied him with boredom. His normally tan skin was pale and sickly beneath his crisp business suit. His shoes were bright white and matched the ivory cane that he leaned heavily on. His dark hair was slicked back as usual, but a few tendrils had stubbornly fallen out of place. His brow furrowed when he realized I was sitting in his chair, and he moved his eyes along me in his usual perverted fashion. When he smiled, it was strained and his fangs elongated against his red lips. He was hurting, and he was hungry. I smiled.

"Titan." His smooth voice flowed out. "What a pleasant and..." He paused, studying me again. "Stimulating surprise."

"Joe," I replied. He leaned heavier on his cane. I figured if he didn't sit down soon, he would be passing out and then I would get no information from him.

I slowly stood and stretched my body. I walked toward my bike stroking the smooth metal and leather. Then I plopped down into the seat and faced him. "Sit down. Let's chat." I crossed my arms and waited. I knew he hated to admit weakness by taking the seat, but I also knew he was more interested in finding out why I was here.

He slowly and stiffly walked to the chair lowering himself down into it. He watched me, "I have to admit my relief in seeing you so... alive." He smiled. "You had me worried, Titan."

"Really? You should know by now that I can handle myself."

His eyes zeroed in on the raised scar that ran along my neck from ear to ear. "So the Titanium Angel has once again escaped death's cold grasp."

I sat back against the dash and handlebars. "I assure you, I escaped nothing."

His brows raised. He sat forward onto the edge of his chair studying me. "You rose again?"

I smiled. This seemed to surprise our audience into sudden silence. His eyes widened and he smiled again. "Like a Phoenix from the ashes."

"Sorry to disappoint, there was no fire, nor warmth. Enough about me. I hear you were in a little tussle recently."

He hissed and sat back. A tension suddenly filled the silent room. His eyes hardened. "That cold bitch had better never darken my doorway again, or I will unleash every vampire within my power onto her and I will show her no mercy." Hisses and snarls raised around the room.

"Yeah. She's not my favorite person either." I raised a brow. "Care to share?"

He smiled. "For some reason she thought that she could get information from me, but she was sadly mistaken. You will be relieved to know that she looks just as bad as I do."

I smiled. He was right. That did make me feel better. "What was she inquiring about?"

He looked at me with surprise. "Why, you the Titanium Angel, of course."

That was surprising. Why would she be looking for information on me?

"I see that I have surprised you, Titan. Perhaps, you would like to know why?" He smiled.

Damn. I was too nosy for my own good. "Perhaps. What do you want?"

He smiled. "I know that you are tracking her. And I know that eventually, you will find her. When you do, you will deliver her here to me. I will be the one to kill her."

I thought about it. The bitch deserved whatever she got from him, the hard part was that I wanted to kill her myself. She had taken from me, and I would never forget it. "I can do that, but I will not promise that she will be whole, healthy, or sane after I get my hands on her."

He smiled. "Deal."

I smiled. "Spill."

"She thought you were dead."

Knew that.

"For some reason she has great interest in your human. She thought that by getting you out of the way she could turn him and change his allegiance to her."

Figured that.

"Apparently, things went wrong. She is frustrated and she seemed nervous because she cannot locate him. She has no idea if he runs, hides, or even breathes. It's driving her mad."

Join the not so fun club.

"Now, to throw another wedge in her plan, she is hearing rumors that you are alive. Imagine how happy she is. She came to me to see if I had any proof that you were alive. She had somehow found out about my interest in you and decided to visit me." His eyes darkened. "I informed her that I hadn't seen you or your human since we had our slight disagreement. She, of course, did not believe me. Demanded to know any information I had on you, as well as any rumors I had heard of you or your human recently."

"And what have you heard recently?"

He watched me. "Oh, rumors fly as they usually do. Some say that the Titanium Angel was finally brought down by masses of demons, vampires, and witches that cut you apart limb by limb. Others say that nothing can take down the Titan. That the stories are false and you hide with your insanity, waiting for the right moment to rise and take revenge for your lover." He smiled. "My favorite, was the story that we had passed to us by another group of vampires. That you and your human were taken captive by a group of the races working together beneath a witch. A witch that is no mere witch. That they murdered you by draining your blood before your lover and murdered him after he watched you die." Goosebumps rose up on my arms as he continued. "They said that she was trying to make the human into something, something that she could control, something that she could keep. That things went wrong. Very wrong. For instead of an obedient watchdog, something monstrous rose that night. Something that she could not control. A mix of the races with no sanity, no allegiance, and nothing to hold it back. For the only person that could hope to control it, she had murdered in cold blood."

"A Forgotten," I whispered. He smiled at me. This was the first time that I had heard what actually happened to him that night. The cold memory came rushing back into me and I tried to push it away.

He nodded. "A Lost One. Just like you." He studied me. "Now the question is, how long will he survive? How long until he realizes that you live, and by then will it be too late?"

The hurt came, it was nothing new to me. I had known all along what I was possibly facing. Now, it was just confirmed. For I had no doubt that the vamps who had passed the story along were the ones that had attacked us that night. He had become a Forgotten. And a Forgotten has no hope. I cleared my head and turned back to him.

"Sometimes, rumors can hold a ring of truth to them."

He nodded. "They can indeed."

I stood. "So, you could possibly say, that we struck a deal or a bargain of sorts."

He stood, watching me carefully as I walked closer. "You could."

"So in the interest of rumors, you could say, that we might have teamed up." Whispers rose around us.

"Are you suggesting that the Titanium Angel and my vampires are in a partnership?"

I held out my hand. "In the interest of rumors." I felt his men rise around us as more tension filled the room. This was a moment that would be remembered for a long time.

He grabbed my hand firmly in his own, "and revenge." His teeth stretched forward as he smiled.

I smiled back. "I am after all, part vampire."

His brows rose in surprise as hisses and whistles surrounded us. He leaned toward me. "Think about it, Titan." My own brows rose. Those were the same words he used when he had mentioned the possibility of me being part vampire. "You went into death as part vampire, part Light Angel and part Dark Angel. Who is to say that when your lost soul became lost once more, it didn't reach out farther?"

Well shit. I smiled and turned back to my bike. I straddled the seat and kick started it. Loud conversations started and whistles flew at me once more.

"Titan?"

I turned back to Joe who stood with a sly smile on his face.

"Do not forget that I am still awaiting a promise of my perfect bride."

I tried not to make a face. "You can just keep on waiting. I ain't perfect and I don't promise shit."

Hope you enjoyed Titanium by Johanna Marie!

Please check out

http://dreambigpublishing.net

for more info on the books in our collection.